I0640565

Great Britain Patent Office, Griffith Brewer, Patrick Y. Alexander

Aëronautics

an abridgment of aëronautical specifications filed at the Patent office from A.D.

1815 to A.D. 1891

Great Britain Patent Office, Griffith Brewer, Patrick Y. Alexander

Aëronautics

an abridgment of aëronautical specifications filed at the Patent office from A.D. 1815 to A.D. 1891

ISBN/EAN: 9783337399337

Printed in Europe, USA, Canada, Australia, Japan

Cover: Foto ©Andreas Hilbeck / pixelio.de

More available books at **www.hansebooks.com**

AËRONAUTICS:

AN ABRIDGMENT

OF

AËRONAUTICAL SPECIFICATIONS

FILED AT THE

PATENT OFFICE

FROM A.D. 1815 TO A.D. 1891.

BY

GRIFFITH BREWER

AND

PATRICK Y. ALEXANDER.

ILLUSTRATED.

LONDON:

TAYLOR AND FRANCIS, RED LION COURT, FLEET STREET.

1893.

PREFACE.

—◆—

OWING to the large number of specifications which have been filed at the Patent Office, it is extremely difficult for inventors of the present day to ascertain if their inventions have been anticipated.

It is hoped that those interested in the subject of Aëronautics will find this work of benefit to them in their researches, though it must not be expected that all the information contained in the specifications is comprised in so small a volume.

In the yearly indexes published by H.M. Patent Office, many inventions are included under the heading " Aëronautics " which do not particularly refer to the subject. This error in the official indexes is partly the fault of inventors who wish to cover an enormous ground under one Patent. Say, for example, an inventor patents a new motor, and states in his specification that the said motor may be employed for driving locomotives, traction-engines, ships, balloons, etc. The Government would probably place that invention under each of the separate titles, comprising the apparatus to which the motor could be applied. No doubt this is the best way to evade unnecessary responsibility in compiling such indexes ; but in a work of this condensed description it would be impracticable to follow their example, as the reader searching for improvements in aërial machines would hardly appreciate a light sprinkling of traction-engines or ironclad war-ships.

Many of the specifications describe inventions which are no doubt impracticable ; some are even ridiculously absurd and are probably the result of dreams. All these, however, are equally included with the ingenious inventions, as in weeding them from the remainder we should make the work incomplete and therefore of little value. Besides, many practical suggestions may be gleaned from the most absurd inventions; and is it not premature to criticize a question which is still unsolved ?

It is to be hoped that so many failures will not deter inventors from still striving to master the great problem of aërial navigation ; for it should be remembered that aërial navigation is not an *impossibility* but only a *difficulty*, which may be mastered by careful study and perseverance.

GRIFFITH BREWER.
PATRICK Y. ALEXANDER.

AËRONAUTICS.

A.D. 1815.   No. 3909.

PAULY, Samuel John, and EGG, Durs.

" AËRIAL CONVEYANCES AND VESSELS."

ROUND bodies being unfit for navigation through a fluid, a
fish-shaped aërostat is employed. The net is attached to a
frame round the lower part of the aërostat, and the belly of
the balloon is attached to this frame by a ribband or other
appendage to enable same to act as a parachute, in case of
the balloon bursting. The car is suspended to the frame.

Wings are described composed of a head-piece playing
backwards and forwards horizontally, and provided with
feathers formed of silk, fixed to one side of a rod by means
of ribs of whalebone. Five of these feathers may form a
wing, and have their silk edges toward the tail. These wings
will draw the air from the nose of the balloon, and drive it
along its sides to the tail, thus causing the forward motion.
They may also produce an upward or downward motion.

The tail is of similar construction to the wings, and any
motor may be employed.

A barrel is suspended below the car, which, when moved
toward the tail, causes the nose to rise, and when moved
toward the nose depresses same; thus the balloon proceeds
upwards or downwards, as the case may be, in an inclined
direction. Water contained in the barrel may be used as
ballast. The inventors state that the aërostat might be
dispensed with.

B

A.D. 1826.   No. 5420.

VINEY, James, and POCOCK, George.

" IMPROVED KITES."

KITES are employed for drawing vessels, etc., or for raising persons in the air.

The peculiarities of these kites are:—They are fitted with joints in the wings and the standard so that they may be folded up. The wings are spread by a moveable distender. There are four lines for controlling their power or diverting their course. Kite after kite may be attached one behind the other, and thus an indefinite power is obtained.

(*Drawing.*)

A.D. 1840.   No. 8337.

POOLE, Moses.   (*A Communication.*)

" OBTAINING MOTIVE POWER FOR THE PROPULSION OF VESSELS, ETC."

THE inventor describes a screw-propeller having from two to twelve blades, which may be set at from one to eighty-nine degrees, according to " the power of wind you have to act against."

This screw is shown in the two sheets of drawings, in conjunction with a boat or car.

(*Drawings.*)

A.D. 1842.   No. 9478.

HENSON, William Samuel.

" MECHANICAL FLYING MACHINE."

THIS invention describes the employment of an " aëro-plane " for mechanical flight.

In the introductory part of the specification the inventor

states :—" If any light and flat or nearly flat article be projected or thrown edgewise in a slightly inclined position,
the same will rise on the air till the force exerted is expended, when the article so thrown or projected will descend;
and it will readily be conceived that if the article so projected or thrown possessed in itself a continuous power or
force equal to that used in throwing or projecting it, the
article would continue to ascend so long as the forward part
of the surface was upwards in respect to the hinder part, and

that such article, when the power was stopped or when the
inclination was reversed, would descend by gravity only if
the power was stopped, or by gravity aided by the force of
the power contained in the article, if the power be continued,
thus imitating the flight of a bird."

It will be seen from this quotation that Henson had a
clear knowledge of the properties of what is now termed the
" aëroplane," and he proceeds to describe a machine in which
an " aëroplane," propelled forward at a suitable inclination
and speed, serves as a support on the air for itself and other
parts connected therewith.

The car or vessel is made with a view to strength and
lightness, and three wheels are situated below to enable it to
run on the ground. On either side of the car is an extended

surface, made of wood framework covered with silk and firmly stayed with wire, so that the two extended surfaces form a trussed beam of great strength and lightness. A horizontal tail, which can be raised or lowered, is employed at the stern, for the purpose of guiding the machine up or down, and a vertical rudder or tail is employed for steering to the right or left.

Two propellers are employed to drive the machine, and the engine and boiler which are to drive the propellers are preferably placed in the bow of the car, as the weight should be placed forward.

The machine is started by running down an incline, at the same time having the propellers in motion, when it will be found to leave the ground, and it may then proceed in any direction.

There should be about one square foot of surface for each half-pound of weight; and the following are the dimensions of a machine of 3,000 lbs.. which the inventor states he was making :—Surface of the main aëroplane 4,500 square feet, tail 1,500 square feet, and the high-pressure steam-engine was of from 25 to 30 horse-power.

This invention created a great stir at the time, and Mr. Henson made a machine, but it was of no practical use as a means of flight.

A.D. 1843.   **No. 9598.**

SUNDERLAND, Thomas.

"Propelling Ships and Balloons."

Screw-propeller having two flat blades attached to the ends of a cross-bar affixed to a longitudinal shaft.

The impact of a jet of steam on the atmosphere is also described as a means of propulsion. The invention is illustrated as applied to ships, for which it seems to be chiefly intended.

(*Drawing*.)

A.D. 1843.   No. 9642.

POTTS, Lawrence Holker.

" APPLICATION OF BALLOONS."

BALLOONS are employed for drawing cars on tension railways, by which means they become of greater utility than heretofore.

A machine is described consisting of treadles, handles, and cranks, for enabling men to utilize all their strength to actuate wings and oars.

(*Drawings.*)

A.D. 1843.   No. 9856.

MOAT, William Crofton.

" AËRIAL LOCOMOTION."

A MACHINE is described to be driven by manual power (though the inventor states he does not limit himself to this power), composed of an oblong framework of wood.

Four men are shown in the drawings turning a crank, which rotates two frames on either side of the machine, carrying four "flappers" each. These flappers act on the air in their downward stroke, but rise edgewise in their upward movement. The flappers consist of rectangular frames covered with parchment, which swing from pins on the rotating frames, and legs are provided for the machine to stand on when on the ground. A rudder is employed to steer the machine.

(*Drawings.*)

A.D. 1847.   No. 11578.

NEWTON, William Edward.   (*Communicated by Dr. Van Hecke.*)

" NAVIGABLE BALLOON."

THIS invention is to enable balloons to take advantage of the

. various currents of air which constantly blow in the same direction, or monsoons, and currents which are variable. These currents not being very deep it is necessary to keep the balloon at a constant height, and the inventor proposes to do this without loss of gas or ballast.

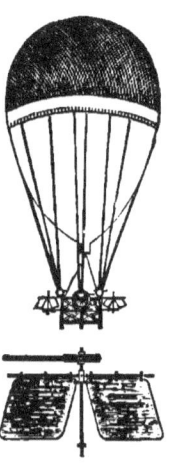

Wings (propellers) are formed of wire rectangular frames, having silk stretched thereon. Two wings are mounted obliquely on each of four spindles, which are rotated by means of hand-wheels, to which they are connected by suitable gearing. When rotated the wings exert a force either up or down; thus the balloon may receive a force of from ten to fifty pounds in either direction vertically, and so be enabled to remain at any desired altitude. If desired, greater power may be employed than that of manual labour.

A.D. 1848.   No. 12337.

BELL, Hugh.

"NAVIGABLE BALLOON AND MECHANICAL FLYING MACHINE."

THIS invention describes two distinct apparatus for navigating the air.

1st. A navigable balloon.

2nd. A mechanical flying machine.

There are also some detail improvements applicable to aërial machines generally, described and shown in the drawings.

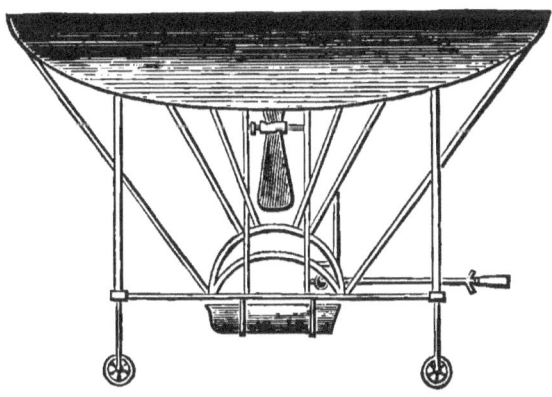

The balloon is made in an elongated form and having a membrane within same, below which latter air can be forced to keep the balloon always distended. The network is made of flat silk bands, which are placed longitudinally and transversely, and also diagonally if required. A single strong band attaches the net to the horizontal circumference of the balloon, which, in case of accident, would allow the lower membranes to rise and fill like a parachute.

A circular valve is held up to its seat by springs and opened by pulling a line.

The balloon is fitted with a framework made of metal tubes, to which the boat-shaped car is attached.

One or more two-bladed propellers are employed to propel the aërostat. Wings having a backward and forward motion in conjunction with a rotary motion are described. Propellers are described which reciprocate, and open and shut like an umbrella, or a hinged double shutter. A water grapnel is made like an umbrella, and having a rope at each end. Dragging it by the rope attached to the "handle" end of the umbrella causes the grapnel to remain full of water, but by pulling the other rope the grapnel is reversed and empties.

For mechanical flight, an aëroplane, having its sides curved downward, is propelled at an angle. Wheels are provided to enable the machine to obtain the necessary velocity, in order to make the ascent. Tubes are employed in the construction of this machine.

A.D. 1849. No. 12452.

BROWNE, John.

"Balloon Railway."

A BALLOON having a car containing passengers is attached by means of a cord to a metal holder, which runs in contact with a rail situated on the ground.

No drawings illustrate this vague specification, which also describes inventions for "wheel-rigged ships" and "atmospheric railways."

A.D. 1852. No. 155.

BROWN, David Stephens.

"Navigating Ships."

THIS invention, although only described as applied to ships, is of interest in aëronautics, for the reason that an aëroplane is employed to take the weight of the ship partly off the water.

The inclined plane may be employed either above the ship or below same. In the first position the plane will act on the air, whilst in the second position the water will be acted on. The ship may be drawn by kites or balloons.

(*Drawing.*)

DE MANARA, Horace.   (*Provisional only.*)

" APPLICATION OF BALLOONS."

BALLOONS are employed to keep seats on vessels in an upright position, in order to prevent sea-sickness, consequent
on the motion of the vessel.

(*Drawings.*)

JOHNSON, John Henry.   (*A Communication.*)

" NAVIGABLE BALLOON."

AN elongated balloon supports a frame carrying the boiler
and engines, which latter drive two pairs of paddle-wheels
and parachute propellers.   The paddle-wheels are made to
act on the air during half their revolutions, the blades being
feathered during the return motion.

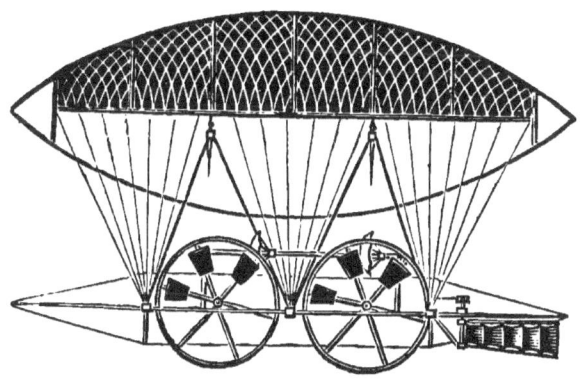

The parachute propellers are mounted on horizontal reciprocating shafts, and open and close alternately, the said
shafts being actuated by eccentrics on the paddle-wheel axles.

Horizontal sails, which may be adjusted to any angle, are
employed to regulate the descent.   Four triangular sails,

fore and aft, prevent rolling by their resisting surface, and the machine may be inclined at any angle by means of two weights, which may be adjusted longitudinally.

A rudder is employed for steering horizontally.

A.D. 1853. No. 395.

DE NORMANDY, Alphonse Rene Le Mire.
(*Partly a Communication.*)

"ARTICLES MADE OF GUTTA-PERCHA."

BALLOONS are made by pouring a certain quantity of gutta-percha into a vessel having its interior shaped to the form of the required balloon. The vessel is turned in every direction until the interior of same is covered with a film of the solution. In drying this film contracts, and may then be removed.

(*Drawing.*)

A.D. 1854. No. 224.

ALDBOROUGH, Benjamin O'Neale Stratford, Earl of.

"AËRIAL NAVIGATION."

IN this most lengthy specification (79 pages) an aërial machine is described having an aërostat of elongated form.

Wings are most minutely described, which are intended to act in a similar manner to those of a bird. These wings are made to rise slowly against springs and then descend almost instantaneously, thus compressing the air by percussion under the concave part of each wing.

Various theories on the flight of birds are propounded by the inventor, and his object has been to imitate these actions with his artificial wings.

A tail is described which may act as a rudder, and strike

downward when the vessel is rising, and so compress the air beneath, as the inventor believes birds commonly do, especially pigeons.

The wings may be employed in a machine without an aërostat.

Any number of persons on board the aërial vessel may work the wings, each person working a separate wheel.

Combinations of canes are used in all parts of the aërostat which require to be kept stiff, or of a sharp or angular form, the strength of each being suitable to its situation, and these strips are sewed to the material of which the envelope is constructed.

Smoke or heated air, with or without gas, is employed, and long chimneys diminish the danger of fire.

Perforated metal or wire-gauze is placed inside the chimneys, which latter may be covered, or partly so, with asbestos cloth.

Vacuum chambers, which can be acted on by currents of air, are described, for admitting the gas from the aërostat when the same has been distended by rare atmosphere at great altitudes, and the aërostat is divided to contain gases of various density.

A "pilot bout" containing as much weight as can be spared from the aërial vessel, such as cordage, provisions, and persons, descends first, and then draws the vessel down by means of cords and two windlasses. Grapnels are also taken in the pilot boat.

A landing-place, having a railway for receiving air-ships, is described, and a building is provided for their reception.

The 24 sheets of drawings are most theoretical in their nature, and it is extremely doubtful if many parts of this invention could be made from the vague though lengthy description.

(*Drawings.*)

A.D. 1854. No. 759.

BOBŒUF, Pierre Alexis Francisse. (*Provisional only.*)

" BALLOONS FOR MILITARY PURPOSES."

BALLOONS are held captive by wires, which may also be employed for signalling or exploding matters in the balloon, from an electric battery situated on the ground.

The gas in the balloon may be used for projecting missiles.

A.D. 1854. No. 1224.

ALDBOROUGH, Benjamin O'Neale Stratford, Earl of.

" LOCOMOTION ON LAND AND WATER."

THE adaptation of wings (described in specification No. 224, A.D. 1854) to navigation on water, land, or ice. Aërostats, combined with vacuum and medium chambers, are also employed.

By exhausting the air in the vacuum chambers and working the wings the vessel may be caused to slide upwards from the water on to the ice ; as, for instance, for the purposes of scientific discovery at the North Pole.

Claim: " The adaptation of the principles and combinations for which I obtained former Letters Patent, bearing date the 30th day of January last, under the title of ' Improvements in Aërial Navigation,' or of modifications of the same, or of certain parts thereof ; and also the other improvements, as herein specified, to the navigation of the water, and also to locomotion on land or upon ice, and to any other purposes to which the same may be applicable."

(*Drawings.*)

A.D. 1854.   No. 1334.

DARTIGUENAVE, Prosper Guilhaume. (*Provisional only.*)

"FLYING MACHINE."

TWO apparatus, similar to parachutes, are placed one above the other, and alternately pulled up and down.

These parachutes are worked by steam or other suitable power, and when the desired height is reached the machine is directed by a horizontal flapper fixed on a centre, which may have an upward or downward inclination given to it by the aëronaut. Wings are provided to enable the machine to turn, their direction being guided by the aëronaut.

A.D. 1854.   No. 2447.

LUFF, Henry James. (*Provisional only.*)

"WAR BALLOON."

A BALLOON freighted with explosive compounds, and having a telegraphic communication with a vessel, is used for attacking forts and towns.

The movements of the vessel can be directed from the balloon, and the movements of the vessel can bring the balloon to any desired position for letting down explosives. Plans of fortifications by photographic process may be obtained from the balloon, which latter may, when desired, be actuated from the land.

A.D. 1855.   No. 206.

JOHNSON, John Henry. (*Communicated by André Marie Préverand.*)

"KITES."

THE kite-frame is composed of two laths crossing at their centres, and capable of being folded parallel to one another.

The textile material which forms the sail portion is permanently secured to the ends of one lath, and temporarily attached to the ends of the other.

The tails are composed of flat boards, through the centres of which the cord passes, the said boards presenting their flat faces towards the wind.

A float attached to a mooring line may be drawn along by a kite ; and for signalling purposes, signals may be attached to the body or other part of a kite.

A number of loops are provided on the " belly-band " of the kite, for attaching the main line, and thus the angle may be varied according to the amount of wind.

(*Drawing.*)

A.D. 1855.   No. 625.

ALDBOROUGH, Benjamin O'Neale Stratford, Earl of.

"AËRIAL NAVIGATION."

IMPROVEMENTS are described on the invention described in specification No 224, A.D. 1854, and forts are described for the reception of aërial vessels.

Various warlike manœuvres with aërial vessels are also described.

This specification, like others by the same inventor, is very lengthy, and no abridgment of same can give any idea of the nature of the invention. Indeed, with the original specification before them, the writers are quite unable to understand how the apparatus is to be manufactured from such vague descriptions.

(*Drawings.*)

A.D. 1855.   No. 1136.

CURTIS, William Joseph.   (*Provisional only.*)

"BALLOONS AND KITES."

GUNPOWDER-GAS is employed to inflate balloons.   Kites or

wings are attached to balloons to enable same to be governed from land or water, and these kites and balloons may propel a ship. Missiles may be conveyed and discharged by an electric spark, conducted along the cords or connections, or the missiles may be discharged by clockwork attached to the balloon.

A.D. 1856.   No. 2062.

ALDBOROUGH, Benjamin O'Neale Stratford, Earl of.

"AËRIAL NAVIGATION."

THIS specification describes improvements on inventions described in specifications No. 224, A.D. 1854, and No. 625, A.D. 1855.

Valves in the outer aërostat admit air to same when the external pressure is great, and air may also be permitted to escape by valves at the stern. Tubes or air-channels in the aërostat strengthen same.

Air-channels in the aërostat assist in steering the aërial vessel, and two separate aërostats may be employed, their lower surfaces acting as wings.

Double curtains protect the passengers and machinery during bad weather ; and improved springs are described for actuating the wings, which latter may also be assisted in their movement downwards by the force of the air contained in the chambers above.

Two pilot boats are employed, and elastic cables are used with the grapnels.

Rotary aërostats may be employed, and the invention may be applied to locomotion generally.

Fourteen sheets of drawings are appended to a seventy-page description, both of which are like other specifications by the same inventor, viz. most vague and theoretical in their character.

(*Drawings.*)

A.D. 1856. No. 2154.

LASSIE, Jean Baptiste Justin.

"NAVIGABLE BALLOON."

THE aërostat is made in a cylindrical form having a projecting helical screw on its outer surface. A smaller cylinder is provided within the aërostat, in which latter the crew walk

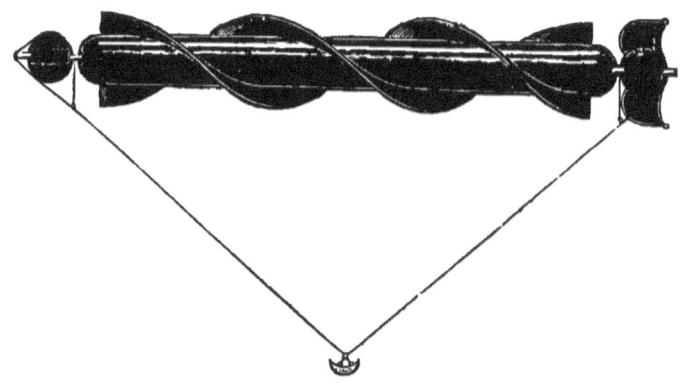

round in a similar manner to convicts in a treadmill. This rotates the whole aërostat, which makes the same advance in the air.

The inventor proposes to make the aërostat 900 feet long, and 90 feet diameter. Three hundred men could be employed, half of which number would be on duty at a time. According to the pitch of the screw, the speed may be fast or slow.

A cut-wind is provided at the bow, and an auxiliary balloon having two vertical blades is employed at the stern for steering.

An adjustable weight is suspended below to regulate the angle of the balloon.

The descent may be performed by pumping air into auxiliary balloons. Spring safety-valves are employed ; and the aërostat may be made of iron, copper, or aluminium.

A.D. 1856. No. 2256.

PELLEN, Marius.

" COATING FOR BALLOONS."

CAOUTCHOUC prepared in England, and subjected to the inventor's mode of preparation, is particularly applicable to the manufacture of balloons.

Varnish is composed of amilaceous substances ; such as enulin, lichen, gum arabic, adragant, mucilage, and vegetable substances mixed with some kinds of gum, sugar, gelatino, dextrine, glucose, albumen, collodion, submitted to a certain preparation " without ether of gelatinous matter, that is, of pure gelatine of fish skin and of glue."

These gums are prepared with pure water diluted with alcohol ; they must be very limpid, and should be strained.

The varnish is applied while the balloons are distended.

Small balloons should be filled at a pressure of about 40 inches of water ; and the varnish above described may suitably be employed for coating the interiors of large balloons.

A.D. 1856. No. 2993.

CARLINGFORD, Godwin Meade Pratt Swift, Viscount.

" FLYING MACHINE."

THE car is in the shape of a boat, and fitted with three wheels beneath same, one being in front and two behind.

Two wings of slightly concave form are fixed to the sides, the sustaining laths of which wings pass through the body of the car from one wing to the other, and thus hold them firmly in position. These wings serve the purpose of an "aëroplane" resting on the air, but having no movement imparted to them. A tail and rudder are provided, and the machine is propelled by means of the " Carlingford screw," actuated by a hand wheel and situated in the bow of the car.

A sustaining surface of 25 to 30 ft. square is proposed,

though the machine may be considerably increased in size to carry very superior weights, in which case, however, the surface need not be increased in the same proportion. This conclusion is arrived at for the reason that an eagle weighing 80 lbs. has only four times the floating surface of a rook weighing one pound.

The machine may be started by suspending the stern end of the car by means of a trigger and cord, to the top of a 9 ft. pole. The bow of the car is connected to two lines passing over pulleys on the tops of two other poles, and a weight is attached to the other ends of these lines. By releasing the trigger, the lines at the bow are pulled forward by the weight descending, and the machine receives a great forward velocity. The machine then becomes free, and speed may easily be sustained by turning the aërial screw.

" I have proved by experiment that an aërial screw of only 5 inches long can give a pull greater than a ten-pound weight suspended to a cord and drawing through a pulley ; and as it will only take such a small force to maintain the flight of the aërial chariot, that what we look upon as fabulous may hereafter come to pass, and that, like the chariot of Jupiter, we may yet behold two eagles trained to draw the aërial chariot.—N.B. This observation may give the witty an opportunity of showing off."

It is not necessary to continually turn the winch or work the pedal for actuating the aërial screw, as the machine can descend on an incline, and thus travel fifty or sixty miles according to the height attained.

(*Drawings.*)

A.D. 1857. No. 1054.

ALDBOROUGH, Benjamin O'Neale Stratford, Earl of.

"AËRIAL NAVIGATION."

THIS specification describes improvements on Nos. 224 and 625, A.D. 1855, and No. 2062, A.D. 1856.

The weight of the crew of aërial vessels and other weight

carried by such vessels, is utilized for producing a rotary motion in the rotary aërostat. The application of the weight is also described to produce an oscillating or vibrating motion, or to operate wings or propellers.

Twin hulls or cars may be employed, in which the advantages of a sharp prow and bluff prow are united.

Curtains form a protection to the aërostat when anchored in an exposed position.

Retractile tubes, projecting downward, warn the aëronaut on approaching the ground ; and the aërostat may be jointed to the car in such a manner that the movements of the aërostat need not be imparted to the car.

(*Drawings.*)

A.D. 1857.   No. 1581.

CLAIR, Joseph Etienne Marie Jean.   (*Provisional only.*)

" PROPELLER."

Two hollow barrels tapering towards both ends and surrounded by screw vanes, on being rotated propel the vessel to which they are connected.

A.D. 1857.   No. 2483.

BALBONI, Pascal.   (*Provisional only.*)

" PROPELLER."

THE fin or propeller is formed by a triangular blade, working through a slot in an axle which receives a rotary motion. The blade receives a vibratory motion at every half revolution of the axle, thus moving towards the bow and performing another half revolution, when the same action is repeated.

This fin, or "aile nageoire," is to supersede the paddle-wheel and screw now used in steam vessels.

(*Drawing.*)

A.D. 1859. No. 2330.

BRIGHT, Henry.

" FLYING MACHINE."

Two propellers are mounted above the car of a flying machine, these propellers being made to revolve in contrary directions.

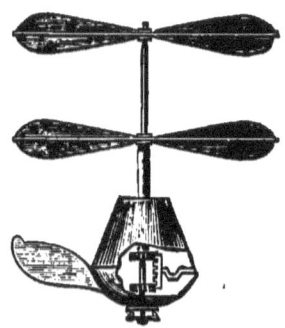

This revolving of the propellers in opposite directions keeps the car from gyration.

The descent is performed by reversing the propellers.

The accompanying illustration shows the principle of this invention.

A.D. 1860. No. 561.

SMYTHIES, John Kinnersley.

" FLYING MACHINE."

A BOILER is described having a number of tubes for obtaining a large heating surface with a small amount of weight.

Vaporized hydrocarbon is burnt, which is formed from liquid hydrocarbon, stored in a tank below the apparatus.

The weight of the water to be carried is also reduced by condensing the steam and employing the said water over and over again. The steam is condensed by passing into a hollow aëroplane formed of oiled silk and stayed by steel rods. The steam condensing in this large condenser runs to the lower part of same and is then pumped back into the boiler.

One or more pairs of wings are employed, which are flapped up and down by an engine, and these wings are made up of large feathers having a rod on one side, the other side being flexible. The rods slightly overlap the flexible edges in such a manner that on the downward stroke the wings beat firmly, with the exception of the last feather which bends to an angle. Thus the main portion of the wing supports the machine vertically, whilst the last feather on each wing gives the forward motion.

The rider steers the machine by leaning in whatever direction he desires to travel, thus changing the centre of gravity. Elastic legs are employed for descending.

(*Drawings.*)

A.D. 1860.   No. 1114.

HENRY, Michael.   (*Communication by Louis Coignard.*)

" PROPELLING AND STEERING."

JET propulsion is described with reference to ships, and the direction of the jet tube is adjustable to enable the force to be exerted in the required direction for steering.

This jet propulsion is also applicable to the propulsion of balloons and aërial vessels, though it is not particularly described as applied thereto.

(*Drawings.*)

A.D. 1860.   No. 1155.

BOYMAN, Richard Boyman.

" MOTIVE POWER."

THIS invention describes the application of the intermittent force of steam to obtain continuous rotary motion.

There is no description of the apparatus as applied to aërial machines, and the inventor merely remarks that the invention may be applied to vessels, locomotives, and aërial machines.

(*Drawings.*)

A.D. 1860. No. 1598.

STEVENS, Charles. (*Communication by C. F. Rablat.*)

"NAVIGABLE BALLOONS."

CIGAR-SHAPED balloon, divided into four compartments, is fitted with wings on either side. These wings are moveable on hinges which form springs, and compartments or valves are situated in the wings.

Pockets are provided, connected by valves to the under part of the balloon, for receiving the gas from the balloon when the same becomes distended. The car is made suitable for navigation on water, and a waterproof cloth inflated with air is attached to its upper edge to prevent the possibility of an upset. Springs are also provided on the under surface of the boat to lessen concussion on landing.

The apparatus ascends or advances according to the velocity given to the wings.

In a modification, the inventor states that the car may ascend by the employment of the wings alone, and without the help of the balloon.

Rudders at bow and stern are employed for steering.

(*Drawing.*)

A.D. 1860. No. 3103.

SILAS, Ferdinand. (*Provisional only.*)

"SIGNALLING WITH BALLOONS."

A CAPTIVE balloon displays various coloured lamps in certain positions, and powerful lights situated below the balloon or on the ground may render the balloon a luminous sphere.

When electric light is employed, the ropes may serve as

conductors from a battery on the ground ; and when gas is the lighting medium, the gas may be conducted through tubes attached to the ropes.

Captive balloons may be employed as lightning-conductors, or as " electro-substractors."

The balloon may be steadied by kites.

A.D. 1861.   No. 492.

JAMES, William Henry.

"APPLICATION OF BALLOONS."

BALLOONS made of strong material are partly filled with water to serve as ballast, and these balloons are then employed for dragging nets or lines with hooks for the purpose of catching fish.

Such balloons may also be employed for saving life from stranded vessels, and also for other purposes at sea.

These balloons are not described with reference to aërial navigation.

(*Drawings.*)

A.D. 1861.   No. 593.

JACOB, Joseph.   (*Communication by Carl Preisenhammer and Carl Weniger.*)

"HYDROGEN GAS."

HYDROGEN gas is made by passing steam through retorts containing metal, such as iron or copper, fired to a red heat. This action decomposes the steam and liberates the hydrogen.

Two sets of retorts may be employed, one set only being in action at a time.

No reference is made to aërial navigation, but this specification is included in this abridgment, because reference is made to same in No. 2377, A.D. 1861, as describing the manufacture of gas for filling balloons.

A.D. 1861.   **No. 1929.**

PONTON D'AMÉCOURT, Gustave Louis Marie, Viscount de.

" FLYING MACHINE."

Two propellers mounted on a vertical axis, one above the other, are situated at the upper part of the machine. These propellers are made to revolve in opposite directions, thus exerting an upward force, ·whilst at the same time one propeller keeps the other in proper equilibrium and prevents the apparatus taking a gyratory motion.

Another propeller is mounted on a horizontal shaft and imparts a forward motion to the machine. Vertical horizontal rudders are provided for steering purposes.

All the propellers are driven from one prime mover, such as a steam-engine, which is situated in the lower part of the apparatus.

This invention is practically the same as No. 2330, A.D. 1859.

(*Drawing.*)

A.D. 1861.   **No. 2377.**

JACOB, Joseph.   (*Communication by Carl Preisenhammer and Carl Weniger.*)

" HYDROGEN GAS."

IMPROVEMENTS are described on the invention set forth in No. 593, A.D. 1861, for manufacturing hydrogen. The retorts for producing hydrogen are made to revolve, or stationary retorts are fitted with trays one above the other, through which the steam is made to circulate.

The iron to be heated is placed on the trays, which iron, if in a finely divided state, can be heated in a few minutes. The steam is then admitted, and passing in contact with the heated iron is decomposed into hydrogen and oxygen, the former being conducted to a condenser and thence to a gasometer, and the latter forms a compound with the heated iron.

Hydrogen thus obtained may be employed for inflating balloons.

A.D. 1861.   No. 2420.

PHILLIPS, Joseph Scott.   (*Provisional refused.*)

" FLYING MACHINE."

THE principle is contained in the propulsion of a plane against the atmosphere by means of wings shaped like the hoof of a calf (or any other animal), affixed to large light wheels, and made of firm or loose flapping and bagging material, the said plane being made of a wooden or iron framework stretched with silk.   The winged wheels being rotated by springs, by hand, or by steam, will flap as they revolve and renew an impulse on the air compressed by the plane, faster than the said air can recede from the pressure, and the machine will be upborne by the air.

The chief part of the invention lies in the rotating wings, which pass on the air in one half a revolution and flap as they pass through the other part.

The inventor probably had some idea of mechanical flight by propelling an aëroplane with feathering paddle-wheels.

A.D. 1861.   No. 2529.

BROWN, David Stephens.   (*Provisional only.*)

" PROPELLING AND SUSTAINING BALLOONS."

AMMONIA and carbonic acid are employed to work engines which actuate propellers for propelling and sustaining balloons.

Condensers containing the ammonia and carbonic acid in a liquid or solid state are suspended from the balloon and borne on the air.   The gases produced are first utilized in the engines and are then injected into the balloon.   Two collapsed balloons are placed in the main balloon to receive the ammoniacal and carbonic acid gases. The balloon is made oblong and has a propeller and rudder at either end. Horizontal fans or screws are placed above the car, which is of boat-like form, these fans being worked by springs which are partly rewound by rotating in a contrary direction during the descent. The car is made inflated, and changes of temperature or atmospheric pressure may be utilized as motive power.

This specification is very vague.

A.D. 1862.   **No. 1786.**

CRESTADORO, Andrea.

" FIRE BALLOON."

THE motive power of a draught, caused by the air-sucking property of fire, actuates a rotary fan-wheel.

A fire-balloon is described in which a stove rests upon a platform, and the chimney terminates in the balloon above.

A motor worked by air-sucking faculty of fire actuates a propelling apparatus.

A.D. 1863.   **No. 867.**

GEDGE, William Edward. (*Provisional only. Communication by Pierre Jacques Carmien.*)

" NAVIGABLE BALLOON."

AN elongated balloon is mounted on a shaft which passes through same from bow to stern. The car is adjustably suspended to the ends of the shaft in such a manner that the angle of the balloon may be regulated. An engine situated in the car propels the balloon by rotating the shaft and balloon, which latter carries sails or a screw thread.

A.D. 1863.   No. 2028.

LÜDEKE, Johann Ernst Friedrich.   (*Provisional only.*)

" SUSPENDING CAMERAS FROM BALLOONS."

A CAMERA is suspended by the rope of a captive balloon, and the exposure may be made by means of an electric current.

A pulley is situated above the camera, over which pulley passes a rope attached to the ground at one end, and to a drum on the ground at the other end.   By this means the balloon may be raised and lowered whilst the camera is kept steady thereby.

(*Drawing.*)

A.D. 1863.   No. 2141.

WELDON, Walter.

" BALLOON."

AN elongated balloon is composed of a number of bags, like the carriages of a railway-train, but with little or·no space between the bags.   These bags should be of greater diameter than their longitudinal length, and the balloon should be of much greater length than its diameter.   The machine thus constructed will float horizontally, and may be propelled and steered.

A.D. 1863.   No. 2959.

NEWTON, William Edward.   (*Provisional only.*
Communicated by Eugene Godard.)

" BALLOONS."

AN improved fire-balloon is described in this specification, and apparatus applicable to fire or gas balloons are also described.

An air-heating apparatus is placed in the car of a " Montgolfier " balloon, and straw or light dry wood is employed to obtain the required heat.   Outer casings, through which air may circulate, are provided round the air-heating apparatus to prevent the radiation of heat inconveniencing the aëronauts, and a fire door communicates with the interior. The fire is supported on a perforated sheet of iron, or a trellis-work of iron bars, and the ash-pan, which is suspended below the

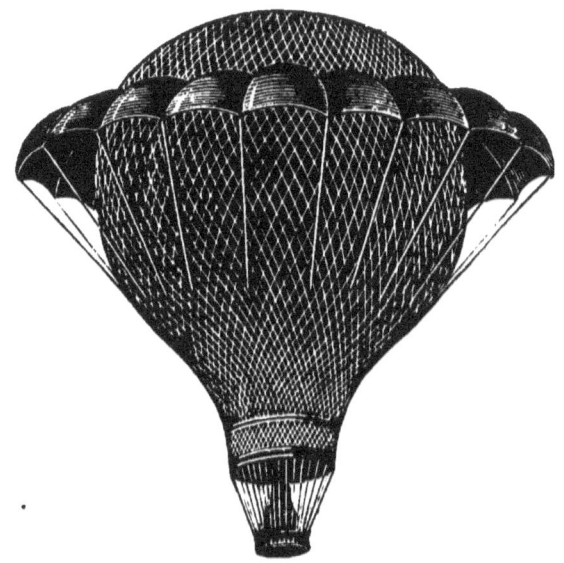

fire, may be raised or lowered to regulate the draught. The air fed to the fire is admitted through a perforated truncated cone, and a similar cone, but inverted, is employed to conduct the heated air to the balloon.

Valves regulate the draught, and a wire-gauze disk prevents sparks entering the balloon. The balloon, which need not be varnished, is covered with straps like an immense net, and a valve may be employed at the upper part of the balloon.

It may sometimes be necessary to empty the balloon more quickly, so for this purpose a cutting instrument is provided in the upper part of the balloon, which, on being pulled by means of a rope, rends the balloon from top to bottom.

To render the grapnel rope elastic, rubber springs are provided, but the rope itself takes the strain when the springs are stretched to their utmost.

A parachute is fitted to the outside of a balloon to prevent rapid descents.

A balloon was made according to the above specification, weighing 4,700 lbs., and having a capacity of 498,500 ft.

A.D. 1863.   No. 3284.

DE SAINT MARTIN, Henry Reda. (*Provisional only.*)

" FLYING MACHINE."

LUNGS having a respiratory action, and composed of two inflatable bags, are employed to give a rising and falling motion to light, rigid frames (wings ?).

A hot-air apparatus supplies the lungs, and also actuates the propelling wheels. The lungs give necessary ascentional momentum to the apparatus, whilst the propellers move same in any required direction.

A.D. 1864.   No. 298.

DAVIES, George. (*Communication by Ferdinand Charles Honoré Phillippe d'Esterno.*)

" FLYING MACHINE."

THIS machine is provided with two wings and a tail, which are moved vertically, horizontally, and torsionally, and the weight of the aëronaut may be altered in position in the car.

The wings and tail are composed of a rigid framework, combined with whalebone strip and a covering of strong silk.

There are hand wheels in the car by which the operator may move the wings or tail in any desired direction.

The inventor has omitted to provide any power for actuating the machine.

(*Drawings.*)

A.D. 1864. No. 591.

BROOMAN, Richard Archibald. (*Provisional only.*
Communicated by Pierre Quentin.)

"CAPTIVE BALLOONS."

Two large balloons are connected to a wire rope in such a
manner that one rises whilst the other descends. The distance
between the balloons should be about 300 yards, and the
people in the cars are protected from the sun and rain.

The ropes which support the balloon, the car, and the
holding rope, are all attached to a spar on which they are free
to turn, the car thus being maintained in a vertical position.

In order to prevent the holding rope coming into contact
with car in windy weather, the end of the rope may be
divided in two and carry a frame in which the car is free to
turn ; or two cars may be attached to the spar, and the rope
attached between them ; or the car may have a recess from
the side to the centre of same, and thus allow the rope to take
any angle without tilting the car.

The balloon is made of strong tarred fabric, lined with tissue
paper, combined with light fabric coated with india-rubber.

The network may be combined with the envelope, and the
envelope thus consolidated terminates in a circular frame
having outlet and inlet valves.

A hyperbolical trunk allows the wind to exert an internal
pressure when the balloon is employed in a hurricane.

A.D. 1864. No. 748.

GEDGE, William Edward. (*Provisional only. Communicated*
by Pierre Jacques Carmien.)

"METAL BALLOON."

A CYLINDRICAL metal balloon with conical bow and spherical
stern, and fitted with sails on its exterior surface, is made to
rotate by means of a suitable steam-engine situated in the car
below.

Two hemispheres, placed at the bow and stern, are blown

into by means of a bellows, actuated by the steam-engines, the air so blown acting as ballast.

Archimedean screws are turned in one or other direction to aid in ascending or descending.

A.D. 1864.   No. 1982.

CLARK, William.   (*Communicated by Alexandre Marie Quinet and Archille Baudouin.*)

"INDIA-RUBBER BALLOONS."

INDIA-RUBBER balloons having an internal valve, which is kept closed by the pressure of the gas within, are described in this specification.

As this only refers to toy balloons, it is unnecessary to deal with the details of this invention.

(*Drawing.*)

A.D. 1864.   No. 2030.

BROOMAN, Richard Archibald.   (*Provisional only. Communicated by Charles Edmond Francois Couturier.*)

"FLYING MACHINE."

EXTENDING arms are fixed at a distance from the body and terminate in wings or flappers.   Springs are fitted at the connection of the wings and arms, and the aëronaut works the flappers by means of cords, and may thus progress even against the wind.

A.D. 1864.   No. 2245.

HAMMOND, Thomas Rundle.   (*Provisional protection refused.*)

"DRAWING BALLOONS."

VULCANIZED india-rubber is distended, and any objects are attached thereto, such as mail bags, boats, waggons, or balloons, which, on being released, are drawn along by the india-rubber.

A.D. 1864.   No. 2299.

MENNONS, Marc Antoine François. (*Communicated by Gustave de Struve and Nicholas de Telescheff.*)

"FLYING MACHINES."

STATIONARY or moveable concave surfaces are employed in machines which fly by mechanical power, the stationary surfaces acting on the principle of aëroplanes, and the moveable surfaces acting as wings.

The first machine, which is designed to carry 120 persons and to move at 30 miles an hour, has a large concave surface attached round the body or vessel for floating on the air. A propeller is provided, driven by a steam-engine, for giving the machine a forward motion, and vertical and horizontal rudders are employed for steering horizontally or vertically. A weighted regulator is provided to maintain the centre of gravity as nearly as possible in the same position. The machine is started down a decline, and when free the engines driving the propeller keep the machine flying.

The second machine is provided with moveable wings, which are actuated by the aëronaut, and the machine is started in a similar manner to the first machine.

(*Drawings.*)

A.D. 1865.   No. 930.

HAENLEIN, Paul. (*Provisional only.*)

"NAVIGABLE BALLOON."

AN elongated balloon, having a horizontal framework around same, is driven by means of a propeller, and steered by a rudder covered with silk. Instead of propellers at the bow, propellers may be situated on either side of the balloon, and mounted on the framework, and a propeller may be mounted on a vertical axis situated below the car for regulating the altitude of the balloon.

The propellers are driven by a gas-engine of particular

construction, having most of its working parts hollow to give lightness, and the gas required is drawn direct from the

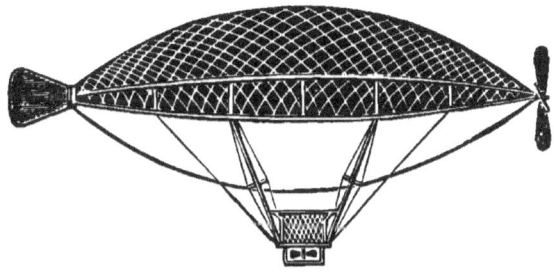

balloon. A small auxiliary balloon, situated inside the balloon, is inflated with air to compensate for the loss of gas.

A.D. 1865.   No. 1037.

ROTHLEB, Gustave Wilhelm. (*Provisional only.*)

"FLYING MACHINE."

A STRONG but light framing surrounds the body of the person who is to fly, and the said framing is prolonged in front and behind about 5 feet. A windrose (having arms like the sail of a windmill) is employed in front, and offers very little resistance to the wind, as it is free to turn on its axis. A revolving wheel, having feathered spokes, acts as a rudder, and the onward motion is obtained by wings which are actuated by spiral springs and by the arms of the person flying. Two elastic reservoirs of hydrogen are attached to the framing to assist in buoying up the person flying in the air.

This provisional specification is extremely vague, and the parts are not very particularly described.

A.D. 1865.   No. 1953.

LAROCHE, Leon Paul. (*Provisional protection refused.*)

" FIRE-ENGINES AND HYDRAULIC MACHINES."

PISTONS of pumps are armed with "conic sharp-edged needle

D

plates, well polished, round, square, and triangular, showing, in one word, all the shapes that have been adopted, to be thoroughly polished and edged."

This principle, the inventor states, may be applied to aërial machines and balloons.

This description is quite incomprehensible, and the inventor who is a native of Paris, probably made his own translation.

(*Drawing.*)

A.D. 1865.   No. 2208.

BONNEVILLE, Henri Adrien. (*Provisional only. Communicated by Charles Edmond François Couturier.*)

" Flying Toys and Parachutes."

A FLYING toy has wings attached to a central body, and a rudder is attached to the hinder part of the body. When the bodies are to fly rigidly, the body, tail, and wings are fixed in the same plane ; but when the wings are to flap they are hinged to the body, which is then inclined downward with the tail in an upright direction. The flapping of the wings is controlled by a thread or other means.

In applying the principle to a parachute the wings would be made of silk, mounted on a suitable framework.

A.D. 1865.   No. 3283.

CLARK, William. (*Communicated by Solomon Andrews.*)

" Directing the Course of Balloons."

THE principle of this invention is propelling and steering balloons during the rising and falling motion, by means of inclined planes.

The specification describes, and the drawings illustrate, three elongated balloons placed side by side, and having their longitudinal equators joined together by a diaphragm. An elongated car is also employed, and the aëronauts, by standing

either in the bow or in the stern, depress the bow or stern of
the balloons, which in rising or falling travel along in the
plane to which the diaphragm is inclined.

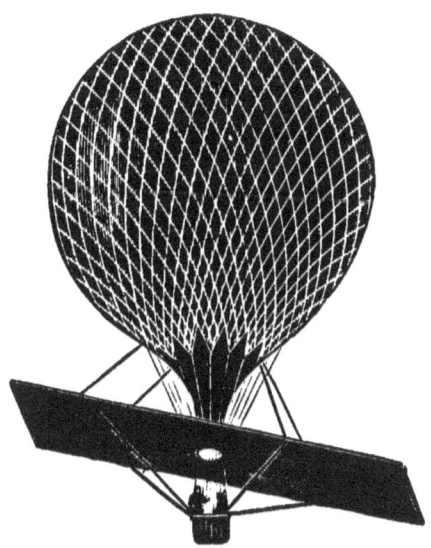

The accompanying illustration shows a plane for the above
purpose fitted to a spherical balloon, which plane may be
adjusted to any required angle.

A.D. 1866.   No. 1143.

BUTLER, James William.   (*Provisional only.*)

"MANUMOTIVE FLYING MACHINE."

AN aëroplane is attached across the shoulders of the person
intending to fly.   The operator imparts an upward and forward
motion to the apparatus by pulling a pair of wings downwards,
the upward motion of the wings being obtained by springs.

The operator, with the above apparatus attached, is conveyed rapidly down a hill on a carriage until the rush through
the air, acting on the aëroplane, lifts him from the carriage,
when by plying the wings vigorously, a flight of considerable
extent may be attained.

The start might also be obtained by jumping from a height, or by being pulled through the air at a great velocity by a rope.

A.D. 1866. No. 1497.

BOYMAN, Richard Boyman.

"PROPELLING VESSELS."

IN this very lengthy specification the inventor describes further improvements in propelling vessels by reaction, which improvements are the result of his experiments on intermittent reaction.

He states that this method will be the only method of propulsion on land, water, and in air.

The invention is not particularly described as applied to aërial navigation, so it is beyond the scope of this book to deal with this particular means of propulsion.

(*Drawings.*)

A.D. 1866. No. 1571.

WENHAM, Francis Herbert. (*Provisional only.*)

"FLYING MACHINE."

Two or more aëroplanes are arranged one above the other, and support a framework or car containing the motive power. The aëroplanes are made of silk or canvas stretched in a frame by wooden rods or steel ribs. When manual power is employed the body is placed horizontally, and oars or propellers are actuated by the arms or legs.

A start may be obtained by lowering the legs and running down hill, or the machine may be started from a moving carriage. One or more screw-propellers may be applied for propelling when steam-power is employed.

A.D. 1866. No. 2489.

BOULTON, Matthew Piers Watt. (*Provisional only.*)

"PROPELLING AËRIAL VESSELS."

A JET of fluid is forced from the stern of the vessel in the direction of the required movement of such vessel. This action imparts movement to the air, which impinges against a curved surface on the stern of the vessel, which is thus propelled. The necessary elevating force of aërial vessels might be obtained by the employment of inclined planes, surfaces, or vanes.

A.D. 1866. No. 2809.

BOULTON, Matthew Piers Watt. (*Provisional only.*)

"PROPELLING AËRIAL VESSELS."

THE invention described in this specification is practically similar to the invention previously protected by the same inventor (No. 2489, A.D. 1866).

A.D. 1866. No. 3262.

BOYMAN, Richard Boyman.

"NAVIGABLE BALLOON."

THE inventor describes at length the state of aëronautical science at date of the application for this patent, and endeavours to show by his arguments that aërial navigation can

never be accomplished by mechanical flight. The opinions of Dr. Pettigrow, the Duke of Argyll, and Dr. Arnott are quoted, but the inventor differs from them, and maintains that aërial machines must displace a quantity of air of equal weight to the entire aërial machine with its cargo.

It is proposed to make a machine having a steel aërostat and weighing in all 600 tons. The aërostat is to be cylindrical with conical ends, 200 feet in diameter, and a quarter of a mile long ; yet the resistance will only be 5070 lbs., and the propelling force 406 horse-power.

Jet-propulsion is employed (viz. propulsion by the impact of a current of air), which may either be produced by a jet of steam, or by a blower of the rotary blower type, which is shown in detail in the drawings accompanying the specification.

The reaction-nozzles revolve so as to propel or back the vessel, and also to act as elevators and depressors.

Rudders are employed, working in pairs, one fore and one aft.

The gas contained in the aërostat may be employed for heating the boilers, though, if preferred, the heating-gas may be stored in separate receivers.

Water is injected into the boiler by a steam injector, which forces the water at a sufficient velocity to overcome the pressure in the boiler.

Moveable ballast keeps the machine at the required angle.

To anyone interested in the science of aëronautics, this specification is well worth careful study ; the reflections, opinions, and theoretical views being most elaborately written and argued by an inventor, who without doubt was a most clever man.

A.D. 1867.   No. 466.

HENRY, Michael.   (*Communicated by Henry Giffard.*)

"Balloons."

An enclosure of the height of a balloon, and having a rounded upper edge, is employed to protect a captive balloon from the wind whilst on the ground. The captive rope passes over a pulley to a steam engine, the said rope tapering in thickness from the balloon downward. A trench is made to receive the car, which latter is suspended from a ring and situated in a cage. The lower part of the balloon is elastic to allow of expansion, and a stuffing-box closes the mouth of the balloon, through which the valve-line passes. Tubes are connected to the neck of the balloon and rise upwards to elbows hung from the net ; these tubes then descend towards the ground, where they are open to the air and act as exits and safety-valves. A tube is connected to the valve at the top of the balloon to enable gas to be admitted from above, and thus expel the heavier gas at the lower part of the balloon. A waterproof covering protects the balloon and net from rain.

(*Drawing.*)

A.D. 1867.   No. 473.

KAUFMANN, Joseph Meyers.

" FLYING MACHINE."

THE car contains the engine and boiler, and is mounted on wheels to enable it to run on land when starting, whilst at the same time the said car can float on water.

The engine actuates the wings, and pillow-blocks are employed to oscillate the wings, so that they may strike the air at an angle both in the up-stroke and the down-stroke, thus wedging or screwing the machine through the air.

Buffers, which may be forced out by steam-pressure, are provided for giving the machine a sudden lift upwards when starting, or the machine may be run along on its wheels until the air acting on suitable aëroplanes, set at an angle, gives the required lifting-power.

A tail and two guides are employed to steer the machine vertically or horizontally.

A tender, carrying stores, fuel, and water, and cars may be drawn behind the above-described machine, in which case the tender and cars would be provided with aëroplanes for supporting them on the atmosphere.

(*Drawings.*)

A.D. 1867. No. 696.

BOULTON, Matthew Piers Watt.
" Propelling Vessels."

This invention refers most particularly to propelling vessels by drawing water by means of a pump, in a direction " opposite to the vessel's advance, and expelling it in the same direction."

Reaction-wheels worked directly by steam may give a rapid rotation to a propeller for the purpose of aërial locomotion.

A.D. 1867. No. 1392.

SMYTH, William.
" Flying Machine."

The car, which is of cylindrical form with tapered ends, is provided with horizontal propellers for propulsion, and vertical propellers for elevating.

Aéroplanes are employed for sustaining the machine, and one pair of these aëroplanes may be extended at the bow and one at the stern, or several pairs may be arranged one above the other, in order to save length and weight.

The propellers are actuated by a motive-power machine, in

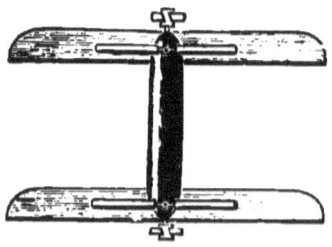

which the explosive force of the combustion of mixed gases is utilized, which explosion expands concertina-like chambers.

A.D. 1867.   No. 1525.

KAUFMANN, Joseph Meyers.   (*Provisional only.*)

" APPARATUS CONNECTED WITH FLYING MACHINES."

THE pressure in the boiler is regulated by a " sneap," which consists of two pistons connected together, one being in communication with the steam, and the other with a mercury-gauge.   At a certain pressure, the movement of the piston allows the steam to escape, and a whistle which is provided warns the attendant.

The flow of oil to the furnace is regulated by a piston, which moves in proportion to the amount of pressure in the boiler ; the piston-rod is connected to a valve, and thus diminishes the amount of oil fed to the furnace on the pressure in the boiler exceeding the amount required.

The inventor also describes apparatus previously set forth in his specification No. 473, A.D. 1867.

A.D. 1867.   No. 1932.

CRADDOCK, Thomas.   (*Provisional only.*)

" FLYING MACHINE."

A SMALL shaft is fixed to the person's body, and rotated by means of clutch pulleys, which are actuated by the feet and hands pulling down cords, the recovery of the pulleys being accomplished by springs.

The rotation of this shaft actuates wings, which receive an up and down, and also a swivel, action, thus pulling the person forward as well as supporting him in the air.

The wings, which are made on the principle of a lady's fan, are intended to move like the wings of a bird.

By employing two or more pairs of wings acting at different times, a continuous power is obtained.

Steam-power may be employed, and as many as 40 wings on each side of the car could then be utilized.

42

A.D. 1867. No. 2115.

BUTLER, James William, and EDWARDS, Edmund.

"FLYING MACHINE."

AN elongated triangular aëroplane is employed, having a web down the centre of its underside, the aëroplane and web resembling in shape a paper dart.

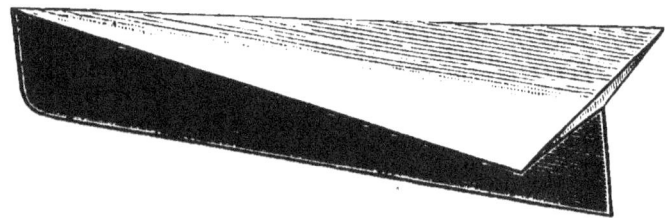

Horizontal and vertical rudders guide the machine vertically and horizontally.

Propellers or wings may be employed for imparting a forward movement to the apparatus, or a jet of steam or other fluid may act by reaction on the air.

When steam-power is employed, the aëroplane may be made hollow for condensing the steam, and thus save weight by using the same water repeatedly.

The apparatus may be started from a carriage running on wheels, and when the speed has become sufficient the air acting below the aëroplane will raise the apparatus from the carriage.

A.D. 1867. No. 2223.

BOYMAN, Richard Boyman.

"PROPULSION."

THIS invention describes, and shows in very clear drawings, further improvements in jet-propulsion; but these improvements being shown as applied to ships, and it being only incidentally mentioned that the invention may be applied to aërial machines, a detailed description would be beyond the scope of this work.

(*Drawings.*)

A.D. 1867.   **No. 2229.**

NELSON, James Edward.   (*Provisional only.*)

" NAVIGABLE AËROSTAT."

THE car is suspended from an aërostat of disc form, having a portion of its centre removed.   By adjusting a weight suspended below the car the apparatus assumes an inclination, and can thus skim through the air in descending.

Sails hinder the passage of air through the central opening of the balloon, thus regulating the velocity of descent ; and rudders steer the machine vertically and horizontally.

In order to obtain a start, the machine is forced vertically upwards out of a cylindrical tower by means of compressed air.

The machine may be propelled by the reaction of a jet or jets of fluid escaping from a reservoir or generator.

A.D. 1867.   **No. 2397.**

GOUCHER, John.

" PROPELLING."

AN apparatus is described for propelling vessels on water, which apparatus, it is stated, is also applicable to propelling aërial vessels, though this application is not particularly described.

Wings or flaps are hinged to a central rib in such a manner that they hold the water if moved in one direction, but fold on the rib if moved in the contrary direction.   These ribs are attached at right angles to rods which connect similar cranks, so that on the rotation of the cranks the flaps hold the water during half a revolution, but are withdrawn from the water on the return half-revolution.

(*Drawings.*)

A.D. 1867.   No. 2504.

SMYTHIES, John Kinnnersley.

" STEAM FLYING MACHINE."

A STEAM bird is constructed, with wings fulcrumed on the
ends of links attached to the body of the apparatus, and these
wings are composed of feathers which act on the air during
their downward stroke, but rise without much resistance,
owing to the feathers deflecting and permitting the air to
pass between same.

The wings are connected at their inner ends to the piston-
rod of a steam cylinder, which in falling and rising flaps the
wings up and down.

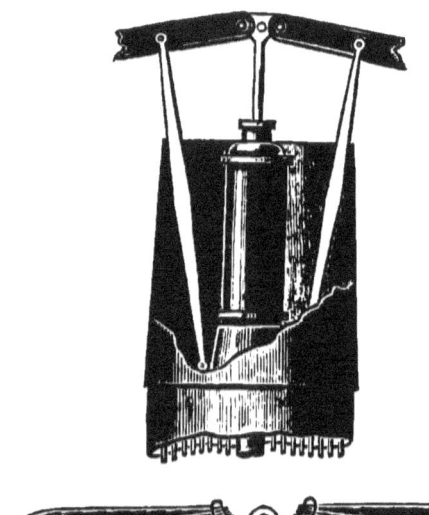

The boiler is constructed with a number of small tubes to
give a large heating surface with small amount of weight, as
well as requiring a very small amount of water ; and the heat

is obtained by burning vaporized hydrocarbon combined with a hot-air blast. The exhaust steam is condensed in a hollow tail, thus saving weight in the quantity of water required. This tail also serves the purpose of a supporting surface (*i. e.* aëroplane).

Minute details are described.

A.D. 1867.   No. 3036.

HENRY, Michael.   (*Communicated by Henry Giffard.*)

"BALLOONS."

THE specification describes improvements on an invention of Henry Giffard's, No. 466, 1867.

Instead of employing an elastic neck, the leading lines are made shorter, thus allowing the balloon to expand or contract without sagging.

Safety-valves are employed at the lower part of the balloon, and the neck is made of a short rigid tube having a flexible end.

A pressure-valve shows the pressure of the gas in the balloon, and the mooring-cable passes through the centre of the car, which latter may have a double bottom for the reception of ballast &c.

The mooring-cable is worked by steam-engines and is fitted with a tension-gauge.

The passengers enter the car by means of a foot-bridge, and an enclosure is provided to protect the balloon from the effects of bad weather.

(*Drawing.*)

A.D. 1868.   No. 392.

BOULTON, Matthew Piers Watt.

"PROPELLING AËRIAL MACHINES."

JETS of fluid are employed as the motive-power of aërial machines. The jet of fluid, steam for instance, issues towards the hinder part of the vessel, which is shaped to offer but small resistance to the air.

Various kinds of jets are described, which may be employed as a supporting power by passing over the upper surface of a plane, thus reducing the pressure on its upper side, or the jets may be employed for propelling aëroplanes at an angle, which thus perform mechanical flight.

Mixtures of inflammable gases may be ignited in a receptacle and thus produce the required jet by its escape through a suitable orifice.

Steam boilers are described having a large heating-surface.

In order to prevent an aëroplane leaving the plane in which it is travelling, self-regulating mechanism is employed, consisting of two rudders and a balance-weight, which mechanism corrects the angle automatically.

(*Drawing.*)

A.D. 1868.   No. 412.

MASEY, Philip Edward.   (*Provisional only.*)

" STEAM FLYING MACHINE."

A SERIES of rotary vanes or blades, mounted on vertical axes, give the required lifting-power, and vanes mounted on horizontal axes impart a forward motion to the machine.

These vertical and horizontal axes are driven by means of a rotary engine situated on a boiler having a large heating-surface.

A.D. 1868.   No. 568.

HULLETT, John.   (*Provisional only.*)

" EMPLOYMENT OF KITES AND BALLOONS."

A ROPE is suspended by kites, situated one above the other. These kites may be adjusted in angle by means of cords and weights. Persons &c. may ascend the rope by means of a sail attached to a spar carried on a frame free to run up the rope on pulleys.

The kite or kites may be fitted with gas-holders, and a balloon may be employed for elevating.

A.D. 1868. No. 1005.

BOULTON, Matthew Piers Watt, and IMRAY, John.

"FLYING MACHINE."

A CYLINDER having two pistons, one working at either end of same, is situated in the body of the machine. The piston-rods are attached to a pair of wings in such a manner that on the pistons being driven apart, one from the other, by the explosion of mixed gases between them in the cylinder, the wings are brought down, thus effecting the flight of the apparatus. The upward movement or recovery of the wings is effected by the natural pressure of air beneath same caused by the weight of the machine.

A secondary piston conveys the inflammable mixture between the two main pistons, and modifications are described of the various parts of mechanism.

The wings are formed of rods curved backwards and covered with light fabric, and these wings are capable of adjustment.

A tail is employed, mounted on a universal joint, thus allowing of its moving vertically and horizontally for the purpose of steering and balancing the vessel.

(*Drawing.*)

A.D. 1868. No. 1178.

SPENCER, Charles Green. (*Provisional refused.*)

" MANUMOTIVE FLYING MACHINE."

THE apparatus consists of a T-shaped web having vertical and horizontal limbs, which diminish to a point at the bow. The horizontal web acts as an aëroplane when the machine is propelled forwards, and there is a receptacle in the vertical web for a man.

By running along the ground the machine becomes supported on the atmosphere, and the person actuating suitable propeller-fins keeps the machine in motion. A rudder may be employed.

A.D. 1868. No. 1666.

HAMMANT, William. *(Provisional refused.)*

"FLYING MACHINE."

THIS provisional specification does not clearly describe any invention, but the inventor states that the apparatus consists of a frame of thin copper hollow cylinders charged with hydrogen.

Elevating apparatus, consisting of fans, whose blades descend flatways and rise edgeways, are provided, and the supporting apparatus is said to consist of wings fitted with feathering blades. Screw-blades are employed for propelling, and the machine may be actuated by any suitable power.

A.D. 1868. No. 1815.

CRESTADORO, Andrea. *(Provisional only.)*

"HOT-AIR BALLOON."

A BALLOON is made of metallic sheet, and provided with a tap at top and bottom. The air inside the balloon is heated by a furnace, whose chimney passes up through the centre and out at the top of the balloon.

The inventor states that the air in a balloon of 200 ft. diameter, heated to 230° F., would have an ascending power of 38 tons.

A.D. 1868. No. 1881.

BOYMAN, Richard Boyman.

"NAVIGABLE BALLOON."

THIS specification describes improvements on the invention, by the same inventor, No. 3262, A.D. 1866.

Instead of employing gas as the lifting power (in navigable balloons made of metal), it is proposed to rarefy the air in the aërostat by exhausting or heating same. Rotary pumps are shown for exhausting, and the machine is propelled by the action of a jet or jets of air on the outer atmosphere. The pumps are set in action until sufficient air is exhausted to give the required lifting power, and the machine can then be propelled in any direction.

When it is desired to descend, air is admitted to the aërostat, which becomes heavier than the amount of air it displaces.

The aërostat is made of rings of metal with a sheet-metal covering to same, and is strengthened internally by stays. Quotations from correspondence between Professor Blanc and the inventor are given at great length.

(*Drawings.*)

A.D. 1868. No. 1987.

NEWTON, William Edward. (*Provisional only. Communicated by C. Williams.*)

"NAVIGABLE BALLOON."

THE balloon is of elongated form, having the under horizontal surface flat. The propellers, which consist of adjustable vanes capable of being feathered, may be employed for propelling, steering, elevating, or lowering the machine.

A rigid platform is attached to the balloon, and the car is attached below the platform by rigid stays. The balloon, with the help of a " stay-hoop," forms a parachute in case of accident, and horizontal adjustable rails act as aëroplanes.

Compressed gas is carried to compensate for leakage, and steam is generated with carburetted hydrogen gas.

Persons may descend to the ground by ladders, when the balloon is anchored, and the balloon need not be brought right down to the ground for this purpose.

A.D. 1868.   **No. 2162.**

LIVCHAK, Josef.   (*Provisional only.*)

" NAVIGABLE BALLOON."

A BALLOON, which is elongated with conic ends, is stated to be driven by the centrifugal force of the moving parts, and also by the application of the resistance of the air. The balloon is covered with an air-tight cloth, the two edges of which are secured to a loose frame connected with the body which carries the steam motor.

The body may have its distance from the balloon modified, and "prismatic casings or wings " are mentioned in this specification.

A.D. 1868.   **No. 2680.**

HUNTER, John Morrison.

" FLYING MACHINE."

AËROPLANES are employed for supporting the apparatus on the atmosphere, and the propulsion is obtained by rocket jets, *i. e.* jets impinging on the atmosphere, which jets are produced by the combustion of gaseous hydrocarbons mixed with atmospheric air.

There are two aëroplanes, one on each side of the vessel,

mounted on their centres so that they may be adjusted in angle, to direct the machine up or down ; and the outer edges of these aëroplanes are provided with jets, pointing downwards, to buoy the machine up when required.

Jets are provided at the stern to propel the machine, or propellers may be employed having jets at the ends of their blades, for giving the desired rotary movement.

By altering the direction of the bow or stern propeller, the vessel is turned on its axis, and so travels to the right or left, or this steering may be performed by steam-jets acting diagonally at the bow or stern.

The machine is started by running down hill on wheels which are provided for that purpose, which wheels are connected to the body by means of springs.

A generator for making gas, and improved jets are also described.

(*Drawings.*)

A.D. 1868.   **No. 3677.**

GRYLLS, Henry William.   (*Provisional only.*)

" SPRING-MOTOR FOR AËRIAL MACHINES."

THIS provisional specification describes a motor to be driven by a spring or springs.

The mechanism is placed in the car of a balloon, and drives a shaft, which projects from the car and carries fans or other driving arrangement.

A.D. 1869.   **No. 1124.**

ABEL, Charles Denton.   (*Provisional only.   Communicated by Emile Jombart.*)

" FLYING MACHINE."

A NARROW platform constructed of a framing of wood and

filled in with louvre boards, laths, or staves is provided with quadrant-shaped wings.

A person can impart an up and down motion to the wings by means of levers.

A.D. 1869. No. 1769.

MICHEL, Marius. *(Provisional refused.)*

"EMPLOYING BIRDS FOR FLYING."

BIRDS are harnessed to a triangular framework, to which latter the car is suspended.

The birds may be guided by means of reins attached to their wings, or rudders may be employed for this purpose.

A.D. 1869. No. 2827.

NOBLE, William Henry. *(Provisional only. Communicated by Frederick Marriott.)*

"NAVIGABLE BALLOON."

AN elongated balloon is divided into three compartments, the bow and stern compartments being for the reception of gas, and the centre compartment for the steam engine.

Aëroplanes which increase in width from the bow to the stern are mounted horizontally on each side of the balloon, and a rudder having vertical and horizontal webs is employed for steering vertically and horizontally.

The balloon does not contain sufficient gas to cause it to rise, but when the propellers are actuated the machine rises with the greatest ease.

A.D. 1870. No. 623.

BOYMAN, Richard Boyman.

"PROPELLING BY REACTION."

THIS invention refers to improvements in propellers for producing jets for propelling vessels and aërial machines by reaction. More efficiency is obtained by employing these improved propellers, which, as in the previous inventions by the same inventor, draw air from the forward direction and eject it towards the stern.

(*Drawings.*)

A.D. 1870. No. 1469.

HARTE, Richard.
" FLYING MACHINE."

THIS machine, which may be propelled by either muscular or steam power, is provided with an aëroplane and propelled by a two-bladed screw. These blades have more of their superficies on one side of their axes than on the other, and they may be regulated in pitch according to the speed required.

Rudders are employed for steering, and wheels are provided to enable the machine to move on land.

A "balancing beak" is employed at the bow of the machine, which, by its momentum, ensures the passage of the front of the machine through the air. The machine may be started down a hill or by rotating the propellers.

(*Drawing.*)

A.D. 1870. No. 2040.

ROSS, William Murray. (*Provisional only.*)
" PROPULSION."

AËRIAL machines are to be raised and propelled through the air by means of apparatus consisting of a number of vacuum-pumps.

Vessels are also to be propelled in a like manner, and locomotives are to be stopped by pistons acting against the air.

(*Drawings.*)

A.D. 1870. No. 3272.

BRANNON, Philip. (*Provisional only.*)

" BALLOONS."

A BALLOON is constructed in three divisions, one above the other, the upper division containing hydrogen and the middle division being fitted with a heating-apparatus for rarefying the air.

Wheels with feathering-gear, or propellers, give propulsion to the machine, and the motive power may be obtained from a tangential fan-wheel driven by currents of air.

Plunging parachute propellers might also be employed, and all the propellers work on universal joints for steering.

A.D. 1871. No. 728.

OSSELIN, François Alfred.

" OBTAINING AND APPLYING MOTIVE POWER."

THIS invention is based on a new law, and the apparatus, which is to be called the " dynamogene," is stated to be both " economical and universal."

The apparatus is described as applied to " ascentional engines " which are of the " general form of a kiosk borne in the air by the statical action of the differential."

The inventor gives a quantity of mathematical formulæ, and states with confidence that by the use of his apparatus the problem of aërial locomotion is solved, but he does not particularly describe the manner of obtaining this much-wished-for result.

(*Drawings.*)

A.D. 1871. No. 944.

BOYMAN, Richard Boyman.

" SHIPS AND PROPULSION."

THE principal part of this invention refers to ships which are made of great length and small cross section, to enable them to proceed at great speed without extra power.

These ships are propelled by reaction, the power being obtained by means of rotary pumps, which pump water in the reverse direction to the movement of the ship. These propelling pumps are also applicable to aërial navigation.

(*Drawings.*)

A.D. 1871. No. 2031.

HUNT, Bristow. (*Provisional only. Communicated by Robert Courtemanche.*)

" AËRIAL MACHINE."

THE machine is of a fish-like form, and propelled by propellers driven by steam-power.

Two screws will be used for ascending, and one screw is situated at the rear end for propelling, whilst the steering is performed with a rudder.

Aëroplanes, which can be adjusted, are provided at the sides of the vessel, and in descending the screws may be stopped and the vessel allowed to descend on an inclined plane.

A foot bridge and four supports are provided, and balloons containing hydrogen are attached to the bow and stern to lighten the ship.

A.D. 1871. No. 2781.

RIEBER, Juan. (*Provisional refused.*)

" NAVIGABLE BALLOON."

A TRIANGULAR balloon is provided with steam-engines for blowing the balloon forward, having one edge foremost to cut the wind. Weathercocks are employed to indicate the direction in which the balloon is moving.

The drawing accompanying this specification would have been more suitable for a comic paper than to illustrate this " supposed " invention.

(*Drawing.*)

A.D. 1871.   **No. 3067.**

WILSON, George.   (*Provisional only.*)

"MOTIVE POWER."

STREAMS of water are forced from a receiver and pass over step-like channels, thus unbalancing the pressure of the atmosphere, and causing it to act at intervals beneath the said channels.

This motive-power apparatus is for performing mechanical work in propelling bodies on the ground or through water, and is also employed for raising bodies in the air.

(*Drawing.*)

A.D. 1871.   **No. 3238.**

MOY, Thomas, and SHILL, Richard Edmund.

"FLYING MACHINE."

AN elongated body for containing the motor and passenger is suspended in the centre of a double hoop framework, which latter is mounted on four wheels for running on the ground when starting the machine.

Two propellers, each composed of eight aëroplanes placed radially on an axis, are situated on either side of the machine. These aëroplanes are altered in their pitch as they revolve in such a manner that on striking downward their forward edges are slightly inclined downwards, whilst in ascending they are inclined upwards, thus always propelling and serving as supports on the air.

Two adjustable horizontal aëroplanes are situated at the stern of the machine to steer same up or down, and these aëroplanes are actuated automatically by a pendulum, or they may be actuated by hand.

(*Drawings.*)

A.D. 1872.   No. 411.

BROWN, David Stephens.   (*Provisional only.*)

" FLYING MACHINE."

Two aëroplanes, which may be double-walled to serve as generators or condensers, are placed at a distance apart and held in position by tubular framework.

The planes may be altered in inclination at rapid intervals, and the propellers may be of the screw, fish-tail, wing, or rocket kind.

A.D. 1872.   No. 821.

SOUL, Matthew Augustus.   (*Communicated by Paul Haenlein.*)

" NAVIGABLE BALLOON."

A BALLOON of elongated form supports a framework, having two propellers mounted horizontally on same. A car containing a gas-engine, and fitted with a vertically mounted propeller below, is attached to the frame, and rudders are attached to the frame at the bow and stern for steering horizontally.

The gas for burning in the gas-engine is drawn from the balloon itself, and an auxiliary balloon situated within the main balloon is provided for the reception of air as the gas is withdrawn.

By driving the side propellers by means of the gas-engine the balloon is propelled forward, and by driving the propeller below the car the balloon may be raised up or down without expenditure of gas or ballast.

A condenser is described in which ether or ammonia is employed for keeping the gas-engine cool.

(*Drawing.*)

A.D. 1872.   No. 3076.

DUTHU, Jean Baptiste.

" STEERING BALLOONS."

SAILS are provided on a balloon to enable it to beat and tack against the wind in a similar manner to a ship. A screw or fan, actuated from the car, is provided to aid " in these evolutions " in such a manner that when manœuvring the proper side may be presented to the wind.

Anchors are provided with two ropes to enable them to hook or unhook at will, the flukes being jointed for this purpose.

A mast and horizontal spars are provided in the balloon, and a spring safety-valve is provided at the top to allow the gas to escape when at a certain pressure.

(*Drawings.*)

A.D. 1873.   No. 2346.

BROWN, David Stephens.   (*Provisional only.*)

" MOTOR."

A STEAM-ENGINE for propelling aërial machines is made to act with great energy at short intervals, instead of in a continuous manner.

Springs hold the piston-rod back until the pressure is sufficient to overpower the springs, which piston then moves with great force.

A.D. 1873.   No. 2776.

MARTIN, Margaret.

" BALLOONS."

A BALLOON or train of balloons of elongated form travels between two points by means of an endless rope to which they are attached. The endless rope passes over pulleys at either end which are worked by steam, and auxiliary balloons may be attached to the rope at intervals to support the weight of same.

This lady inventor proposes to run a balloon line in this manner from Dover to Calais, the rope being suspended about 400 feet above the sea.

(*Drawing.*)

A.D. 1873.   No. 3309.

FLEURY, Albert.   (*Provisional only.*)

" STEERING PARACHUTE."

IF a weight be attached to a rectangular plate by cords of equal length connected to the corners of the plate, such plate in falling will be pulled down vertically. Should, however, the cords be of unequal length, the plate will travel down on an incline, or if the weight be omitted and a balloon employed in its place the balloon will rise on an incline.

This principle may suitably be employed to convey torpedoes of considerable weight under water, by weighting them to descend at an angle. On arriving at the bottom a weight is unhooked and they rise at an incline towards the ship. Flying-birds, fishes, &c., may also be made in this manner.

A.D. 1873.   No. 4154.

VAUGHAN, Edward Primerose Howard.   (*Communicated by Edward Clarence Morse.*)

" ADVERTISING BALLOONS."

CAOUTCHOUC balloons are ornamented or otherwise marked by means of stencil plates. The marking or colouring materials may be applied to a balloon whilst inflated or uninflated, and the balloon may also be marked internally.

A.D. 1873.   No. 4255.

GAVEAU, Jean Charles.

"Navigable Balloons."

Two or more balloons of equal capacity are connected by a framework, which forms a vessel with a deck and lower frame.

A screw propeller is driven by mechanism which is not described, and a mast and sails are provided for directing the apparatus in case of need.

(*Drawing.*)

A.D. 1873.   No. 4279.

BROWNE, John Collis.

" Propelling Balloons."

A SCREW propeller, composed of two pairs of blades, is employed for propelling and assisting to raise balloons, such blades being constructed so as to act separately on the fluid.

The propeller-shaft is provided with a universal joint to enable same to be directed in any direction.

This propeller is also described as applied for raising water, ventilating buildings, &c.

(*Drawing.*)

A.D. 1874.   No. 81.

DE VOGT, Henric Christian.

" Flying Machine."

A FRAME or wing, nearly horizontal and slightly convex in form, constitutes the elevating and propelling means. This frame is strengthened by struts and stays, and is fitted with feathers which overlap one another, thus holding the air on the downward stroke, but opening to allow the air to pass between same on the upward stroke.

A reciprocating up-and-down motion of this frame is obtained by the direct action of a piston-rod, and a rudder having vertical and horizontal vanes is employed for steering vertically or horizontally.

A boat carries the boiler and engine, and a kite is fitted ·round the boat to prevent rolling.

(*Drawing.*)

A.D. 1874.   No. 777.

RIDLEY, Joseph Douglas. (*Provisional only.*)

" FLYING MACHINE."

WINGS are reciprocated by means of a piston actuated by explosions, the motion being imparted through the medium of a piston-rod and cross-piece.

The explosive agents in the cylinder are ignited by an electric spark ; and a tail is provided for steering the machine.

A.D. 1874.   No. 1144.

MÉNIER, Jean Sebastien Anacharsis.

" FIRE BALLOONS."

FIRE balloons are provided with circular burners fed with hydrocarbon from tanks situated in the car.

Asbestos wicks are employed in the burners, and the fuel is partly burned in the form of vapour. The fabric of the balloon may be rendered fire-proof, and the chimney for conducting the heated air to the balloon is provided with a wire spark-guard.

A special carriage is employed for transporting the balloon and its appurtenances in readiness for inflation ; and when inflated the balloon may be held captive to the carriage by a wire rope.

(*Drawing.*)

No. 2808.

MOY, Thomas.

" FLYING MACHINE."

THIS invention relates to improvements on the invention described in specification No. 3238 (1871).

The machine is placed at a suitable angle to the horizontal, and the fixed aëroplanes at the hinder part of the machine, supporting part of the weight, reduce the angle of flight as the speed of the machine increases. The pendulum adjusts the revolving aëroplanes, and steering may be effected by altering the angles of the aëroplanes while in motion.

The machine can be mounted on pontoons or wheels, to adapt them for resting on water or land when at rest.

A pendulum regulates steam or other valves, which actuate mechanism for regulating the angle of a balancing plane, which latter keeps the machine at the desired angle.

(*Drawing.*)

A.D. 1874. No. 2821.

BAGGS, Isham. (*Provisional only.*)

" BALLOONS."

HYDROGEN is generated in suitable generators, by the action of hydrochloric acid or zinc.

In inflating fire-balloons the products of combustion are caused to pass through layers of wire gauze.

Wings are attached to a framework surrounding the balloon, which wings being inclined at an angle cause the balloon to travel on an incline when rising or falling. These wings are so balanced that they take the required angle by the pressure of the air up or down.

A tail is employed for steering.

An arrow is shot into soft ground to anchor the balloon when landing.

A.D. 1874.   No. 3058.

LAKE, William Robert.   (*Communicated by William Frank Browne.*)

" HYDROGEN APPARATUS."

A PORTABLE hydrogen generator is described in which steam is passed through retorts over incandescent material, and from thence through a condensing-coil.
(*Drawing.*)

A.D. 1874.   No. 3132.

SIMMONS, Joseph.   (*Provisional only.*)

" FIRE BALLOONS."

THE chimney is placed on a fire-proof seat and is attached within the balloon.

The car is provided with wheels, and the fuel, which is contained in separate vessels, is raised to the car by force-pumps.

A.D. 1874.   No. 3177.

HIME, Frederick.

" NAVIGABLE BALLOON."

THE balloon is of elongated form and supports three cars, one below for balancing the balloon, and one at each end.   A propeller is mounted on a hollow shaft running longitudinally through the balloon, such shaft being supported at the centre as well as at both ends.

A rudder is employed at the bow for steering the balloon.
(*Drawings.*)

A.D. 1874.   No. 3831.

WATT, Alexander.   (*Provisional only.*)

"Balloons."

Balloons are composed of air-tight chambers in the form of segments of a circle, or the so-called quarters of an orange.

Chambers for generating hydrogen by the action of acid on zinc are described.

A.D. 1874.   No. 3996.

ALEXANDER, Edwin Powley.   (*Provisional only.
Communicated by Stanislas Ludovic Brion.*)

"Navigable Balloon."

Inclined or helicoidal wings or blades are attached round the exterior surface of an elongated balloon, in such a manner that on the rotation of the balloon on its longitudinal axis it is propelled through the air.

The balloon is rotated from the car, which latter is oblong, and is suspended from the axis of the balloon by light frames.

The car is furnished with a screw propeller of its own, and one or more balloons may be combined with one car.

A.D. 1875.   No. 140.

CAVE, John O'Connell.   (*Provisional only.*)

"Flying Machine."

Two shafts, one mounted within the other, carry screw propellers at their upper ends. The lower propeller is of greater size than the upper propeller, in order to overcome the downward current of air caused by the rotation of the latter, or the lower propeller may be revolved at a greater speed.

By varying the angle of the propeller-shafts, the machine may be propelled in any direction.

The steering is effected by a rudder which may also act as a drag.

For military purposes, the machine may be actuated by a compressed-air engine, which is supplied with compressed air from the ground by means of a suitable tube.

A.D. 1875.   No. 169.

CLARK, Alexander Melville. (*Communicated by Ferdinand Charles Honoré Philippe d'Esterno.*)

"KITES."

KITES are employed for suspending a person in the air for military purposes.

The kites, which, if desired, may be provided with a frame, are held in tension from the ground by three or more ropes instead of one rope as has hitherto been the case.

(*Drawings.*)

A.D. 1875.   No. 289.

SIMMONS, Joseph, and MORRIS, Joseph Matthew.
(*Provisional only.*)

"PURIFYING GAS."

HYDROGEN gas is purified by passing it through a mixture of lime and water contained in a gasometer.

The gas thus purified is rendered more expansive and lighter, and is particularly applicable to balloons.

A.D. 1875.   No. 574.

BOULTON, Matthew Piers Watt.

"GENERATOR."

A GENERATOR of small weight in proportion to its power is heated from a combustion-chamber, in which a jet of petroleum and a jet of oxygen meet and are burnt.

The flame thus produced is passed into a chamber where a spray of water is playing. The spray is converted into steam, which, mixed with the products of combustion, is fed from the generator to the engine.

(*Drawing.*)

A.D. 1875.   No. 1690.

MÉNIER, Jean Sebastien Anacharsis.

" Balloons."

THE inventor states that by the employment of aëroplanes attached to balloons the descent or ascent may be made on an inclined plane, thus propelling the balloon.

Rudders steer the balloon, and the car being adjustable the centre of gravity may be changed at will.

A.D. 1875.   No. 2428.

SIMMONS, Joseph.

" Kite."

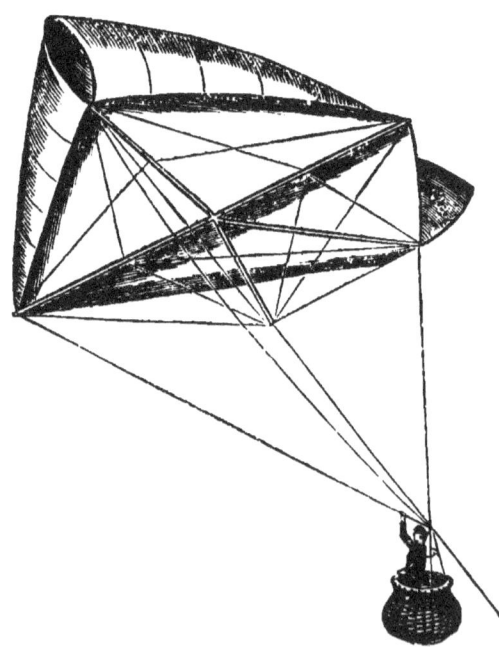

A KITE, composed of fabric strengthened by means of a net

and stretched on a framework, is employed for raising a car containing an aëronaut.

The kite becomes a parachute should the rope break.

A.D. 1875.   No. 2901.

BIDDLE, Daniel.   (*Provisional only.*)

"Sails for Balloons."

Sails supported by a mast and yard-arms are employed for steering balloons.

A.D. 1875.   No. 2979.

McKEE, Henry.   (*Provisional only.*)

"Balloons."

A hot-air balloon is suspended by a wire rope to a gas balloon, and by regulating the heat in the hot-air balloon the ascent or descent may be effected.

A speaking-tube is employed for communicating between the cars attached to the two balloons.

Captive balloons are kept inflated by the combustion of gas fed up through a tube from the ground.

A.D. 1875.   No. 3315.

JENSEN, Peter.   (*Provisional only.   Communicated by Edward Vidal.*)

"Navigable Balloon."

An elongated balloon is provided with two sets of fans (propellers) mounted on the same vertical axis and propelled in opposite directions.

Similar fans are employed for propulsion, and a steam engine is employed for working the fans, which engine is supplied with steam generated from a mixture of carbonic acid with alcohol, or other appropriate substance. Buffers are provided for landing.

This specification is not at all clear.

A.D. 1875. No. 4151.

SMYTHIES, John Kinnersley.

" FLYING MACHINE."

A VERTICAL multitubular boiler, in which liquid hydrocarbon is employed as a heating agent, generates steam for actuating an engine. The piston-rod of the cylinder is connected to the inner ends of two wings which are fulcrumed on the extremities of two links, and by the rising and falling of the piston the wings are flapped up and down.

The steam is condensed in the tail of the apparatus, whence it is pumped back into the generator.

The wings, which are built up of overlapping feathers, hold the air on the down stroke, but not on the up stroke.

(*Drawings.*)

A.D. 1875. No. 4523.

SANDERSON, John George Emilius. (*Provisional only.*)

" PROPELLER."

SEMI-CIRCULAR or semi-oval flat surfaces are attached to a horizontal shaft at an angle of 45°, and this apparatus is employed as a windmill. The inventor, however, states that it may also be employed as a propeller either in water or air.

A.D. 1876. No. 327.

BUCHANAN, John. (*Provisional only.*)

" PROPELLING."

AIR or gas is forced into a chamber which is heated by a steam-jacket. The compressed air or gas thus heated expands, and by escaping through suitable valves propels or steers a balloon by its impact on the atmosphere.

A.D. 1876.   No. 439.

SNOW, Josiah John.   (*Provisional only.*)

"KITE PARACHUTE."

A PARACHUTE is fastened to a short tube, and an elastic spring in the parachute tends to keep it open against a frame until a large pressure of wind acts against the parachute.

The apparatus, being placed on a kite line, runs up same by means of the wind acting under the parachute, but on arriving at the desired height it is suddenly stopped, and the extra force of the wind collapses the parachute, thus allowing the apparatus to run back down the kite-line to the starting-point.

(*Drawing.*)

A.D. 1876.   No. 2393.

RUNKEL, Marc.   (*Provisional only.*)

"BALLOONS."

THE altitude of the balloon is regulated by compressing the gas into a reservoir contained in the car. By compressing the gas the balloon descends, and by allowing the compressed gas to escape into the balloon from the reservoir, the ascent is effected.

The balloon is propelled by projecting a weight horizontally from the car. The weight is connected to another weight below the balloon by a cord, which passes over a pulley, and the weight in being projected hoists the second weight up to the car. When hoisted the second weight may be projected, and in its turn effect a similar result.

A.D. 1877.   No. 603.

MÉNIER, Jean Sebastien Anacharsis.   (*Provisional only.*)

"AËRIAL TOY."

AN india-rubber balloon is supplied with a bird's head, two wings, and a tail, which being fixed to the body of the balloon render same a self-steering aërial toy.

Balloons are to be used as mediums for advertising.

A.D. 1877.   No. 924.

BALLENI, Henri, and PAYNE, John Webber.

(*Provisional only.*)

"NAVIGABLE BALLOON."

WINGS or flappers are attached to a framework situated above a balloon.   The wings are worked by means of rods from the car below, which latter is provided with a motive-power engine.   A horizontal shaft running through the balloon carries a propeller on its rear end, and the car is provided with a rudder for steering.

A gas generator and exhauster are employed for regulating the pressure in the balloon.

A.D 1877.   No. 1406.

MOY, Thomas.

"BOILERS AND ENGINES."

BOILERS for aëronautical purposes are composed of a number of fine curved tubes connecting tubular reservoirs, thus giving a large heating surface with small amount of weight.   Gas or petroleum is employed for heating the boiler.   The feed-water is controlled by a self-acting valve.

Single-acting engines are described which have but a small number of working parts, and as direct an action as possible.

(*Drawings.*)

A.D. 1877.   No. 1647.

WOODBURY, Walter Bentley.

" BALLOON PHOTOGRAPHY."

A PHOTOGRAPHIC camera is suspended to a balloon, which is held captive by a rope containing three insulated wires.

A tail is provided to keep the balloon in its proper position.

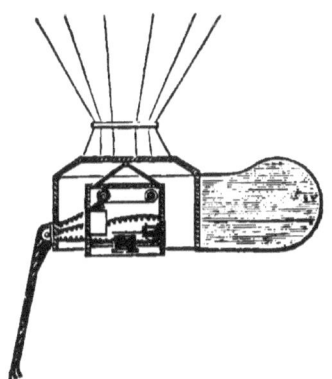

A current passing up by the first wire causes a clockwork apparatus, attached to the camera, to actuate rolls holding the sensitive film in such a manner as to bring a fresh portion of the film behind the lens after an exposure has been made.

A current through the second wire actuates the shutter, and the third wire acts as the return in both instances.

A.D. 1877.   No. 2313.

LAKE, William Robert. (*Communicated by Count Antoine Apraxine.*)

" BALLOONS."

AN annular balloon is mounted on a framework, and is of sufficient size to sustain the maximum weight to be raised.

An auxiliary balloon is provided above the main balloon, and the car is suspended from the main balloon framework.

A rope passes from the auxiliary balloon down through the main balloon to the car below.

The inventor states that by pulling the small balloon down by means of this rope a descent can be effected without loss of gas.

(*Drawing.*)

A.D. 1877.   No. 3814.

ROGERS, Charles Ogle.   (*Provisional refused.*
Communicated by Alfred W. Gittens.)

" AËRIAL BATTERY."

A SHEET of canvas, or a sail or kite with one or more balloons, is held captive from a suitable apparatus on the ground.

Rockets propel the apparatus ; and projectiles, explosive bombs, and nitro-glycerine are conveyed up the rope and dropped into hostile fortifications.

Many other suggestions are made, but not particularly described.

A.D. 1877.   No. 3974.

BRANNON, Philip.

" FLYING MACHINE."

A SUPPORTING surface, termed the "arcuate," is formed of any discoid, inverted ship or boat shape, "or any domic or pyramidal configuration, or other roof form, so as to act both for ascension and propulsion by its concave inferior surface in producing the greatest possible concentric or inward pressure on the adjacent air."

Rotary propellers of various forms are shown and described, as are also their connections and their adjustment in various directions.   Treadles and hand-wheels are in some cases provided for actuating the propeller and rudders, and their connections are also described and shown in the drawings.

For short journeys stored power is employed, or the apparatus may be worked by an air engine or steam engine, in which a lamp-furnace, mass-furnace, flare and guard, or jury furnace may be employed for obtaining the required heat.

An aërostat may be attached to the upper part of the aëroplane if desired.

Many details are described to which the inventor gives his own names, but their number is too great and their forms are too vague for description in this abridgment.

(*Drawings.*)

A.D. 1878.   **No. 513.**

JACKSON, William.

" Navigable Balloon."

Propellers are mounted horizontally and vertically in the car of a balloon for the purpose of propelling and regulating its altitude. The propellers may be worked by hand or by other suitable means or mechanical contrivances.

The balloon proper may be formed in the shape of a bird or other design, and thus be suitable for places of amusement.

A.D. 1878.   **No. 939.**

HEATHORN, Thomas Bridges.

" Jet Propulsion."

Balloons are propelled and steered by the action of a jet of fluid being ejected from the stern end of the car or other

74

part. The orifice through which the jet is ejected is elongated or +-shaped, thus forming a flat sheet of fluid which is more effective than a jet of a similar quantity of fluid projected through a cylindrical orifice.

A fan or blower is employed for obtaining the draught, and any suitable power is employed for actuating the said fan or blower.

(*Drawing.*)

A.D. 1878.   **No. 943.**

ATKIN, Robert. (*Provisional only.*)

" Aërial Vessel."

A vessel formed of thin metal, cane, or wood, covered with silk, is propelled by means of propeller-blades driven by a gas engine or other motor.

The propeller-blades are carried on a hollow shaft, through which steam may circulate, and the vessel is steered horizontally and vertically by rudders.

A.D. 1878.   **No. 1328.**

HADDAN, Herbert John. (*Communicated by Frederick Augustus Lehmann and Charles Ritchel.*)

" Navigable Balloon."

The altitude is regulated by means of a propeller mounted on

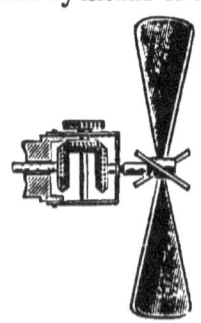

a vertical axis, and a forward or backward movement is imparted to the machine by a propeller mounted horizontally.

The latter propeller is mounted in such a manner that it may be directed to the right or left for steering purposes.

A.D. 1878.   No. 1827.

HADDAN, Herbert John. (*Communicated by Richard William Cowan and Charles Pagé.*)

"NAVIGATING BALLOONS."

BALLOONS are propelled by paddle-wheels composed of a number of paddles, which are capable of turning on their pivots, and thus in rotating either cut through the air or hold same. Each paddle is provided with a projection, and on the paddles being rotated the projection comes in contact with a bar, which turns the paddle at right angles. The paddles are thus always feathered or edge on the wind, except when held in position by the bar, so that on rotation they only hold the fluid in one direction.

The paddles may be made to act in any direction by adjusting the bar, and thus the balloon may be propelled up or down, or in any other direction.

(*Drawing.*)

A.D. 1878.   No. 2039.

VAUGHAN, Edward Primerose Howard. (*Communicated by Count Antoine Apraxine.*)

"BALLOONS."

Two balloons are employed together, and by regulating the distance between them the inventor believes the altitude may be regulated.

This invention is very similar to one previously described, by the same inventor.

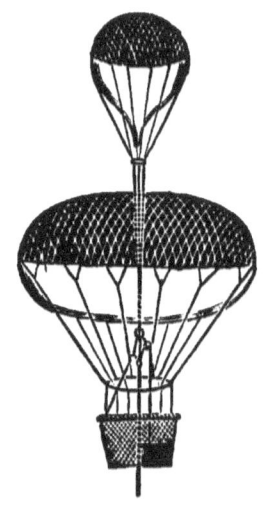

A.D. 1878.   No. 2421.

SAMPLE, James.   (*Provisional only.*)

"PROPELLER."

A PROPELLER for aërial machines is constructed with blades shaped like the wings of a bird, which reduces the slip of the propeller in the air.

A.D. 1878.   No. 3228.

BREWER, Edward Griffith.   (*Provisional only.
Communicated by Eugene Ernest Egasse.*)

"HYDROGEN GENERATOR."

VESSELS and other appliances are described for making hydrogen gas, and the apparatus may suitably be employed for generating hydrogen for inflating balloons.

It is also suggested to carry a small hydrogen generator in the car of a balloon, for generating hydrogen to replace the natural loss of gas.

A.D. 1878.   No. 3546.

ATKIN, Robert.   (*Provisional only.*)

" AËRIAL VESSEL."

THIS provisional specification describes a similar invention to No. 943, A.D. 1878, by the same inventor.

A sheet of drawing is added, showing screw propellers, rudders, and a car which is attached to the vessel.

(*Drawing.*)

A.D. 1878.   No. 4104.

KESSELER, Carl.   (*Communicated by Wilhelm Raydt.*)

" BALLOONS."

CAPTIVE balloons are inflated from a reservoir containing compressed gas. When the balloon is no longer required it is drawn down and the gas is returned to the reservoir by the help of a force-pump.

(*Drawing.*)

A.D. 1878.   No. 4268.

SMYTH, James Stewart.   (*Provisional only.*)

" BALLOON RAILWAY."

BALLOONS are employed for supporting weights to be transported on rope railways. The balloon can either be hauled by ropes, or advantage may be taken of a favourable wind.

A.D. 1878. No. 4332.

NEWBOLD, Henry. (*Provisional only.*)

" BALLOONS."

AUXILIARY balloons are provided connected by suitable valves to the lower part of a main balloon. When the gas expands it passes into the auxiliary balloons, and is thus prevented from escaping into the air.

Hydrogen may be generated by chemical reaction.

A.D. 1878. No. 4757.

JACKSON, William.

" BALLOONS."

THIS invention refers to further improvements on No. 513, A.D. 1878, by the same inventor.

A free balloon is propelled and regulated in altitude by screw propellers, it is also provided with a cannon for projecting a harpoon-like grapnel into the ground for anchoring purposes. Canvas bags, fastened to the car, are inflated for keeping same afloat should a descent be made at sea.

Trapezes are provided suspended to captive balloons, and a safety net is suspended below.

(*Drawings.*)

A.D. 1879. No. 409.

ABEL, Charles Denton. (*Communicated by Julius von Binzer and Eduard Bentzen.*)

" PROPELLERS."

SCREW propellers for propelling bodies through air are built up of a number of S-shaped sections, the centre of the S forming the boss of the propeller.

(*Drawings.*)

A.D. 1879.   No. 594.

BREWER, Edward Griffith.   (*Communicated by
Eugène Ernest Egasse.*)

" HYDROGEN GENERATOR."

THIS invention is a repetition of that described by the same
inventor in his provisional specification No. 3228, A.D. 1878.
(*Drawing.*)

A.D. 1879.   No. 1207.

DILLON, Thomas Arthur.

" ELECTRIC LIGHT ON BALLOONS."

BALLOONS are employed for signalling by electric light. A
dynamo on the balloon is operated by compressed air conveyed to the car by means of a tube, or the compressed air
may be carried in strong receptacles.

A.D. 1879.   No. 1569.

BUCKHAM, William Peruano.   (*Communicated by
James Stewart Smyth.*)

" BALLOON RAILWAY."

WEIGHTS are transported along a rope by the aid of a balloon,
which sustains or partly sustains the said weights.
(*Drawing.*)

A.D. 1879.   No. 2229.

PEARSE, Edward Arthur.

" NAVIGABLE BALLOON."

AN elongated conical-ended balloon is constructed of sheet
copper strengthened externally by stays. A silk gas-bag is

provided in the interior of the copper cylinder, which bag on being inflated expels the air from the cylinder.

A frame, having sleigh-shaped runners, carries the car, which is suspended to the balloon by spring attachments.

Gas engines in the car actuate a pair of screw propellers, which, when driven at a uniform speed, drive the balloon straight ahead, but by altering the speed of these propellers the machine may be driven to the right or left.

The steering up or down is effected by means of an adjustable weight, and spirit-levels are employed to indicate the angle of the apparatus.

The car can be adjusted in relation to the frame, and spring buffers are employed for deadening the shock on alighting.

(*Drawing.*)

A.D. 1879.   No. 2376.

BREAREY, Frederick William.

"FLYING MACHINE."

AN elongated body pointed at both ends contains the requisite machinery and the passengers.

Flexible lever-arms extend on either side, and a flexible spar extends from the tail end of the body. Silk or other suitable fabric is extended from the arms and along the spar at the tail, thus giving a large supporting surface.

Vibrations are imparted to the arms, which propel the machine by a wave-like motion.

The inventor does not mention how the said motion is imparted to the arms.

A.D. 1879.   **No. 3779.**

WISE, William Lloyd.   (*Communicated by William Augustus Leggo.*)

"AËROPLANE BALLOON."

An elongated dart-shaped aëroplane is formed of a double skin to receive gas.

The aëroplane displaces sufficient air to nearly support its entire weight, and also the weight of the car.

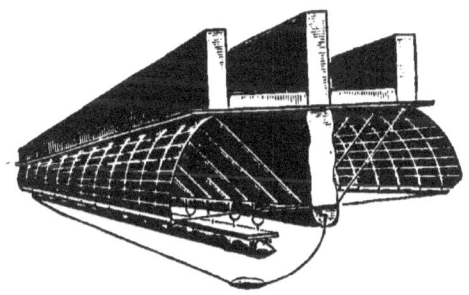

By heating an expansion-chamber the entire machine is made to displace more air than its entire weight, and thus has a lifting power. The centre of gravity is adjusted by means of a moveable weight, and the angle of the aëroplane can thus be adjusted and cause the ascending or descending force to propel the machine ahead.

A.D. 1879. **No. 3997.**

SIMON, Henry. (*Communicated by George Baumgarten.*)

"Navigable Balloon."

The balloon is composed of four component parts, and the car is suspended close up to the lower part of the balloon by means of a rope, which passes through the interior to various ropes and bands on the outer envelope.

A rope-ladder is provided up through the balloon to enable the aëronaut to ascend to the upper part of same when desired.

The apparatus is propelled by means of a two-bladed feathering paddle, which takes a quarter turn at each half revolution, thus alternately holding and cutting through the air. The altitude is regulated by means of a propeller, the blades of which are adjustable in pitch.

(*Drawing.*)

A.D. 1880. **No. 985.**

LAKE, William Robert. (*Communicated by Albert Livingstone Blackman.*)

"Navigable Balloon."

A FIRE-PROOF elongated balloon is made rigid by an internal framework of thin metal tubing, and the interior is divided

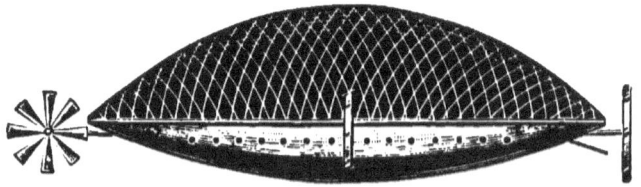

into separate partitions. The hull of the air-ship extends the full length of the balloon.

Propellers are employed for propelling the balloon horizontally, and a propeller which can be adjusted in its angle is employed for steering the machine in any desired direction.

A.D. 1880.   **No. 1776.**

HILL, Micaiah.   (*Provisional only.*)

" NAVIGABLE BALLOON."

A FISH-SHAPED balloon is propelled by compressed air, which is allowed to escape by suitable orifices, situated about one third of the length of the balloon from the head.

A flexible tail is employed for steering.

A.D. 1880.   **No. 4701.**

BONNEVILLE, Henri Adrien.   (*Communicated by Anton de Schuttenbach.*)

" BALLOONS."

BALLOONS are constructed in the form of " an open parachute," thus, in case of the balloon bursting, the parachute prevents an accident occurring.

The balloon, which is constructed of several reservoirs, has the underside of stronger material than the upper side, so that the upper side would burst before the lower.

An air cushion is provided to deaden concussion on landing.

" Mechanics-antagonistical power " is employed for propulsion, obtained by helices actuated by steam-engines. (This part of the specification is not very clear.)

(*Drawing.*)

A.D. 1880.   **No. 4839.**

HIME, Frederick.

" FLYING MACHINE."

Two sets of rods are mounted on axes on either side of a suitable framework. The inner ends of these rods are connected to the cranks situated on a common shaft running down the centre of the machine. The rods are covered with suitable fabric, and thus form a wing on either side.

The cranks are arranged spirally on the shaft, which latter in revolving imparts to the wing a wave-like motion, thus propelling the machine.

(*Drawing.*)

A.D. 1880.   **No. 4871.**

STEVENSON, Robert. (*Provisional only.*)
" FLYING MACHINE."

BODIES are propelled or lifted in the air by a revolving fan, which exhausts the atmosphere in front of the machine or above same, and thus drives it forwards or upwards.

A.D. 1881.   **No. 122.**

MARTIN, Thomas. (*Provisional only.*)
" CAPTIVE BALLOON."

A SMALL balloon without a car is held captive by a rope, and kept vertical by guys attached to its major diameter.

A balloon to carry the passengers has a light tubular guide through same, which passes round the captive rope of the small balloon, and the main balloon can be let up or down the rope by means of a guide-rope connected to the ground.

A stop may be provided to prevent the balloon ascending too high, and the rope may be marked to indicate the height from the ground. An adjustable clip may be employed to arrest the balloon at any elevation on the rope.

A.D. 1881.   **No. 430.**

CAPEL, Thomas John, and DE LA PAUZE, Alfred.
(*Provisional only.*)
" FLYING MACHINE."

THE car or boat is constructed of a framework of light weldless steel tubing, or of bamboo, stayed or trussed together.

This framing is covered with oiled silk or other suitable covering.

A large aëroplane is balanced on a mast situated in the car, and the said aëroplane can be inclined either up or down.

Propellers are mounted on ball-and-socket joints, and can thus be employed for steering as well as for propelling. The car is mounted on springs connected to wheels, and the machine, when started on a level road, rises on the aëroplane being inclined upwards.

A.D. 1881.   No. 807.

WIRTH, Frank.   (*Communicated by Eduard Goehrung.*)

" NAVIGATING BALLOON."

A FRAME composed of tubes carries a car and is suspended by cords to a balloon.   A shaft is mounted horizontally in the frame, the outer ends of the shaft being bent at an angle in the same direction.   Two sleeves are provided on each end of the shaft, the said sleeves being connected by bevil wheels at the bent portions of the shaft, and being provided with discs at their other ends.   Four radial arms are attached to each disc, the arms on one disc being connected to the corresponding arms on the adjoining disc by blades, vanes, or flexible material.   By rotating the sleeves with their discs, the arms, rotating on different axes, are close together at one part of their revolution, and far apart at the opposite portion of their revolution.

The larger surface exposed acts more forcibly on the air than the smaller surface, and by adjusting the bent shaft the larger surface may be made to act in any direction, and so be employed to propel or regulate the altitude of the balloon.

The propellers may be driven at different speeds one to the other, and thus be employed for steering the balloon.

(*Drawing.*)

A.D. 1881.   No. 1195.

BREWER, Edward Griffith.   (*Communicated
by Auguste Debayeux.*)

"NAVIGABLE BALLOON."

AN elongated balloon is propelled by rarefying the air in front
of same.   This is done by rotating a fan at the bow of the
balloon, and any suitable power may be employed.

Auxiliary fans may be employed for governing the move-

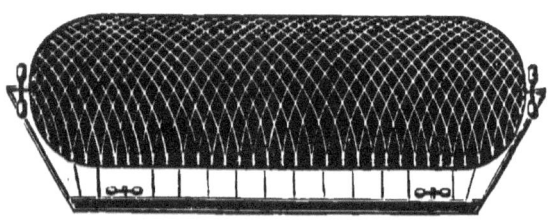

ments of the balloon, and rudders may be employed for
steering.

By this principle of propulsion the balloon is not forced
against the wind, but a path is opened in same into which
the balloon passes without resistance.

A.D. 1881.   No. 1710.

VAUGHAN, George Edward.   (*Communicated
by Count Antoine Apraxine.*)

"BALLOONS."

BALLOONS are regulated in their altitude without loss of
ballast or gas by the employment of ballasted or buoyed
parachutes.   These parachutes by being pulled up or down
relieve the balloon of weight or lessen its lifting power.

Propellers mounted on vertical axes are also employed for

a like purpose, and oscillating beams, which are provided

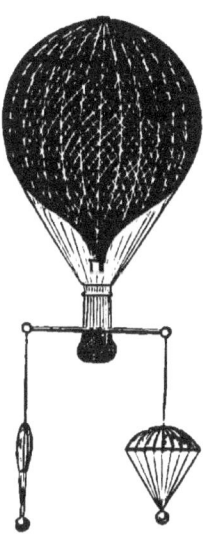

with vanes to hold the air in one direction of the stroke but not in the other, may also be employed.

A.D. 1881. No. 1879.

HUTCHINSON, William Nelson.

" BALLOONS."

THE elevation of balloons is regulated by tightening the envelope, and thus compressing the gas.

The net is extended below the balloon and drawn together at the zone by pulleys, thus compressing the balloon. Elongated balloons are compressed longitudinally by a rope which pulls the balloon together telescopically.

Various other means are described for compressing balloons, and vanes may be employed to prevent gyration.

(*Drawings.*)

A.D. 1881.   No. 3401.

JOHNSON, John Henry.   (*Provisional only.*
Communicated by Gaston Tissandier.)

"Propelling Balloons."

An elongated balloon is propelled by a screw propeller, driven by an electro-dynamic motor, which is supplied with electricity from a secondary battery.   The electric spark which is generated is enclosed by wire netting to prevent danger from fire.

By employing electricity, the weight of the balloon remains constant, and the danger of fire which exists in propelling balloons by steam is obviated.

A.D. 1881.   No. 3561.

VAN de KERKHOVE, Auguste Henry, and SNYERS, Theodore.

" Flying Machine."

Propulsion is effected by the impact of fluid on air or water, which fluid escapes through an orifice, which is preferably of conical form.

An aëroplane is connected above a long vessel which floats on water.   By propelling the vessel and setting the aëroplane at an angle, the vessel will rise and travel through the air.

(*Drawings.*)

A.D. 1881.   No. 3691.

BLACKMAN, Albert Livingstone.

" Navigable Balloon."

An elongated balloon is provided with one or more propelling

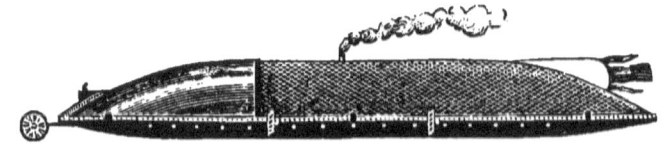

screws at each side, and a steering-screw situated either fore or aft, or at both extremities of the balloon.

Machinery for changing the direction of the propellers is

provided, and a governor is employed for keeping the vessel on an even keel.

A framework is provided to keep the balloon rigid, and the chimney from the generator passes up through the balloon.

A.D. 1881.   No. 4684.

KINNEAR, Frederick Constantine.

"SIGNALLING BALLOONS."

ELECTRIC or other lamps are attached to a framework below a balloon, and such lamps throw light on the surface of the balloon for advertising and signalling purposes.

Electric currents or gas may be conveyed from the ground by wires or pipes. In free balloons the electric current is supplied from the car.

(*Drawing.*)

A.D. 1881.   No. 4887.

EDWARDS, Edmund. (*Communicated by Julio Cezar Ribeiro de Souza.*)

"NAVIGABLE BALLOON."

A TUBULAR framework, attached to the lower part of an elongated balloon, carries aëroplanes, a tail, a screw-propeller, and a steam-engine for actuating the latter. The steering is effected by raising the aëroplanes on one side of the balloon, and depressing them on the other side.

(*Drawing.*)

A.D. 1882.   No. 31.

LAKE, William Robert.   (*Communicated by Carl Wolfgang Petersen.*)

" BALLOONS."

INSTEAD of employing a valve at the top of the balloon, the gas is ejected through the neck by compressing the balloon by means of a reefing-line.

An aëroplane is attached between the balloon and the car for ascending or descending on an incline; or the balloon may be flat at top and bottom to act as an aëroplane for a like purpose.   Disc-shaped rudders are employed, and several flat balloons may be coupled one above the other.

Gas is generated in a suitable apparatus, situated in the boat or car, to compensate for the necessary loss of gas from the balloon.

An indicator shows the inclination of the vessel, and a train of air-ships may be coupled together.

(*Drawing.*)

A.D. 1882.   No. 34.

SMYTHIES, John Kinnersley.

" FLYING MACHINE."

TWO wings are fulcrumed to the sides of a light steam

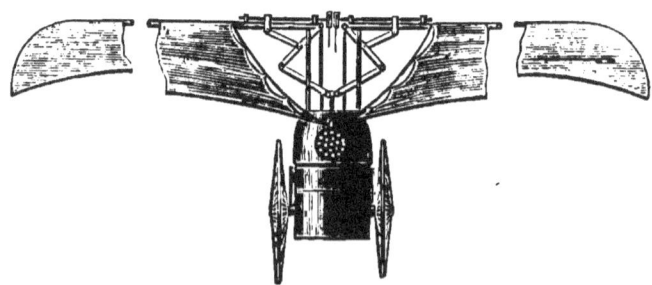

carriage, and these wings are flapped up and down by the action of a steam-cylinder.

Benzoline vapour is burnt to generate steam in a multi-tubular boiler.

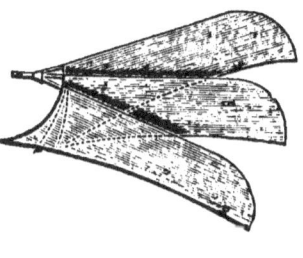

A.D. 1882.   No. 1229.

LAKE, Arthur Wellesley. (*Communicated by Thaddeus Hyatt.*)

"FLYING MACHINE."

A FLYING machine is described in which a rotary fan is mounted in the bow, and two small fans are mounted on either side.

The blades of these fans, which are made of hollow hardened rubber frame-pieces covered with silk, propel and support the machine without the aid of a balloon or other supporting surface.

This invention is based on a law of flight discovered by the inventor.

(*Drawing.*)

A.D. 1882.   No. 1737.

BOULT, Alfred Julius. (*Provisional only. Communicated by Jules Jouanique.*)

" BALLOON."

THE balloon, which is preferably constructed of aluminium, is stated to be made in three parts, though two only, the upper and the lower, are described.   The upper part is somewhat smaller than the lower part, and these two parts are held together by a gallery or framework. The lower part carries a deck, which supports all the appliances required for a journey.

By filling the upper part with gas, the balloon will ascend ; and by pumping gas from the upper to the lower part, the balloon will descend.

A rudder is provided for directing the balloon, but the inventor does not state how this operation is performed, except that the rudder is to be revolved.

A.D. 1882.   **No. 1772.**

WILKINS, Frederick.   (*Provisional refused.*)

" BALLOONS."

TRAINS of balloons, cigar, fish, kite, cylindrical, and other shaped, are mentioned ; which may be propelled by fins, wings, paddles, or be pulled by horses.

Numbers of other vague improvements are suggested, but not particularly described.

A.D. 1882.   **No. 2509.**

BOULT, Alfred Julius.   (*Provisional only.
Communicated by Adolph Werner.*)

" BALLOONS."

BELLOWS-LIKE balloons are attached to a board, and a number of brackets attached to the underside of the board carry shafts with propellers.

Parachute wings and additional propeller-shafts are mentioned, but the invention is not very particularly described.

A.D. 1882.   **No. 4098.**

FISHER, Joseph Alfred, and SPENCER, Charles Green.

" FIRE BALLOONS."

THE lower part of a hot-air balloon is made of asbestos, and the upper part is made fire-proof by the application of a solution of silicate of soda, tungstate of soda, or by asbestos paint.

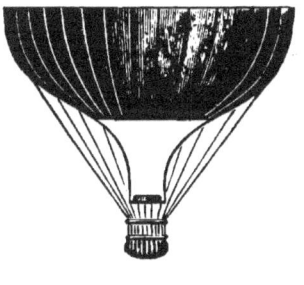

A.D. 1882.   No. 4387.

GREEN, Upfield.   (*Provisional only.*)

"BALLOON RAILWAY."

BALLOONS and aëroplanes are to be drawn along by means of a drum, which takes up a rope, situated on the ground, as the machine travels along.

A.D. 1882.   No. 4585.

MAUGHAN, Benjamin Waddy, and WADDY, Samuel Danks.

"PROPELLER."

A PROPELLER, which can be employed for aërial navigation, has its blades adjustable in such a manner that they may be adjusted in pitch whilst the propeller is in motion.

The surface of the blades, which are concave in form, may be roughened to increase their efficiency.

(*Drawings.*)

A.D. 1882.   No. 4954.

TEMPLER, James.   (*Communicated by Henry Elsdale.*)

"BALLOON PHOTOGRAPHY."

SMALL balloons are employed to support a photographic camera for taking views of ground below the balloon.   When the balloon is held captive, an electric current may be employed to effect the exposure of the plate ; when the balloon is free an automatic apparatus is employed.

A.D. 1882.   No. 5251.

    JENSEN, Peter.   *(Provisional only.   Communicated by Gustav Koch.)*

             " NAVIGABLE BALLOON."

FEATHERING paddle-wheels are arranged in recesses in a cigar-shaped balloon, the said paddle-wheels being capable of revolving at different speeds for steering purposes.

    A number of suggestions are made which are not particularly described.

A.D. 1883.   .   No. 518.

    LAKE, William Robert.   *(Provisional only.   Communicated by Eugene F. Falconnet.)*

             " NAVIGABLE BALLOON."

THE balloon, which is elongated in form and divided into chambers, is constructed of a metal framework covered with a thin metal or other suitable covering. Screw propellers, situated on the sides and also aft, are employed for propelling the balloon, and a screw is provided at the bow for steering purposes.   •

    The internal frame of the balloon is strengthened by braces, trusses, and girders.

A.D. 1883.   No. 1552.

    MAUGHAN, Benjamin Waddy, and WADDY, Samuel Danks.

         " FLYING MACHINE AND MOTOR."

AN engine is described which derives its power from the combustion of solid, liquid, or gaseous explosives, the said engine being of very light construction compared with the power developed.

Two discs or wheels mounted on the same centre are made to rotate in contrary directions by the force of explosions acting between abutments on one wheel and valves on the adjacent wheel. By causing a number of explosions to take place during each revolution a steady power is obtained.

Two or more machines are employed for feeding and firing the explosive, which latter may be composed of a chain of gunpowder-cylinders, one cylinder being exploded at a time.

A flying machine is described having four vertically mounted propellers, two of which are driven in one direction by one wheel of the motor, and the two other propellers are driven in the contrary direction by the second wheel of the motor.

(*Drawings.*)

A.D. 1883.   No. 1824.

DE TELESCHEFF, Nicolas.

"NAVIGABLE BALLOONS."

AN elongated balloon is made with a longitudinal channel through same from end to end. This channel decreases in size at about the centre of the balloon, and thus the resistance encountered in front of the balloon is utilized to assist in propelling same, by the expansion of the air in the rear half of the channel.

(*Drawing.*)

A.D. 1883.   No. 2264.

SJÖSTRÖM, PER.   (*Provisional refused.*)

"FLYING MACHINE."

THIS machine is not very clearly described, and the inventor proposes to use many appliances, which, however, he does not particularly describe.

Screws made of frames covered with canvas are employed, and the blades of these screws can be varied in pitch.

A.D. 1883.   **No. 2715.**

WELLNER, Georg.
" BALLOON."

A BALLOON is made in a wedge form and provided with a neck on its lower side. A stove is provided in the car attached to the neck of the balloon, by which means the temperature may be regulated for ascending or descending.

The balloon takes an inclined force by reason of its angular form acting on the air in the ascent or descent.

A rudder is employed for steering.

(*Drawing.*)

A.D. 1883.   **No. 4055.**

IMRAY, Harold.   (*Communicated by Edouard Oppikofer.*)
" PROPELLING AËRIAL MACHINES."

THE propelling force of the momentum of a moving body is employed in aërial machines, such propelling force not taking its point resistance from the outside air.

The apparatus can be driven by steam or other power, which reciprocates the weight backwards and forwards.

(*Drawings.*)

A.D. 1884.   **No. 7.**

SMYTHIES, John Kinnersley.
" FLYING MACHINE."

THIS machine is of the type previously patented by the same inventor, in which two wings are flapped up and down by the piston-rod of a steam-cylinder.

The wings may have a rigid front edge and a flexible back edge, and they are arranged to hold the air on the down stroke, but not on the up stroke. This may be accomplished by shortening the wing, or allowing the air to pass through the wing, or deflecting the wing at an angle of 30° or 40° during the up stroke, and allowing the said wing to return to its normal position and hold the air during the down stroke.

A large tail may be employed to steady the machine, and if made double-skinned, it may be used as a condenser to condense the exhaust steam. The machine is guided by the aëronaut changing his position and thus altering the centre of gravity.

(*Drawings.*)

A.D. 1884.   No. 2057.

LAKE, William Robert. (*Communicated by François Folacci and Paul Bertin.*)

" NAVIGABLE BALLOON."

A GIRDER is suspended by means of a net from an elongated balloon, the ends of the girder being turned up and connected to the ends of the balloon.

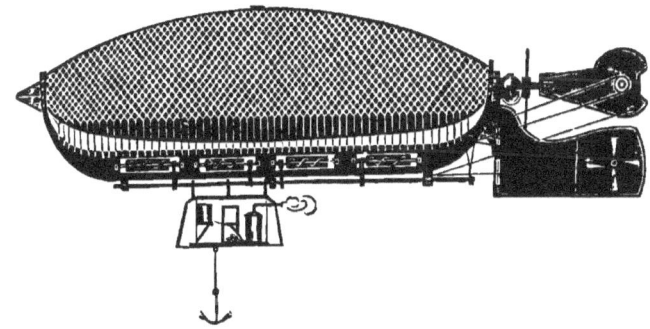

Screw propellers rotate in cylindical casings situated in the girder, and a fan, which is mounted on a universal joint at the stern of the balloon, directs a current of air against an adjacent surface.

The said fan, it is stated, assists in propelling the balloon and the steering is effected by a double rudder operated by steering-cords.

A.D. 1884.   No. 2339.

QUARTERMAIN, William.

"Flying Machine."

A FLYING machine is actuated by a motor in which the power of gases generated from vegetable products is employed; thus dispensing with the weight of a separate generator.

Wings are actuated by cranks and connecting-rods to a crank-shaft, and are feathered on their up stroke, when they also propel the machine forward.

(*Drawings.*)

A.D. 1884.   No. 2469.

HADDAN, Herbert John.   (*Communicated by Otto Hartung.*)

"Navigable Balloons."

A LIGHT frame carrying the propelling screws is suspended from an elongated balloon, and the propeller-shafts being adjustable allow the propellers to steer as well as propel the balloon.

A pair of propellers are mounted on vertical axes, and turntables or wheel-tracks are employed for altering the position of the propeller-shafts.

The propeller-blades are stayed with wires to prevent their lateral deflection.

(*Drawings.*)

A.D. 1884.   No. 2589.

CORNELIUS, William.

"Flying Machine"

Two wings are fulcrumed on the free ends of a U-shaped

frame, and a seat is provided within the frame for the aëronaut, whilst he actuates the wings by handles attached to the inner ends of their rods.

A hinged tail of an inverted trough form is attached to the rear of the frame, and may be actuated by cords attached to the feet of the aëronaut.

A.D. 1884.   No. 2628.

BALLIAN, Serkis-Bey.

"Navigable Balloon and Parachute."

A FLAT balloon is caused to travel on inclined planes in ascending and descending. The underpart of the balloon is made with an umbrella frame, and may be employed as a parachute without the rest of the balloon.

A rudder is employed for steering.

(*Drawing.*)

A.D. 1884.   No. 2879.

DUFF, Robert Low.

"Captive War Balloons."

CAPTIVE war balloons are employed for attacking and defending fortifications and the like, projectiles and explosive bombs being conveyed up to the balloon by a rope and discharged on to the hostile force.

(*Drawing.*)

A.D. 1884. No. 5621.

WIRTH, Frank. (*Communicated by Eduard Göhrung.*)

" PROPELLER."

A PROPELLER for aërial navigation is composed of a paddle-wheel having four blades mounted on a shaft, the said blades being partly enclosed by a casing.

(*Drawings.*)

A.D. 1884. No. 11301.

GOWER, Frederic Allen.

" WAR BALLOON."

THE valve at the top of a balloon is connected to a valve in a ballast-tank by a wire in such a manner as to automatically discharge gas or ballast in order to keep the balloon at a predetermined altitude.

An explosive agent is released at a given time from the balloon by the burning of a fuse.

(*Drawing.*)

A.D. 1884. No. 11994.

HILFREICH, Francis.

" NAVIGABLE BALLOON."

AN elongated balloon is provided with two cars, which are connected together by means of a gangway.

Feathering paddles are attached to each car, the said paddles being constructed of a rod having a blade at either end at right angles one to the other.

These paddles are caused to revolve and also to turn on

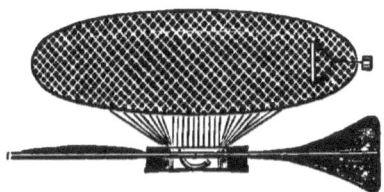

their axes ; and the steering is effected by rotating the paddles at different speeds.

A.D. 1884.   No. 12503.

SMART, George Edward.

" PROPELLERS."

PROPELLERS with hinged blades or wings are employed for aërial machines, the blades opening out during the power stroke and contracting during the return stroke.

(*Drawings.*)

A.D. 1884.   No. 13768.

PHILLIPS, Horatio Frederick.

" BLADES FOR DEFLECTING AIR."

BLADES having curved surfaces are employed to deflect upward the air that comes in contact with their forward edges.

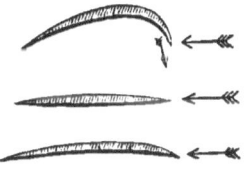

A vacuum is formed over the blades, thus aiding the air below to support the weight.

A.D. 1884.   No. 14038.

ARMOUR, James.

" FLYING MACHINE."

PAIRS of wings are hinged to a spring blade and actuated by
manual power, each pair of wings consisting of a main wing
and a supplementary wing, all of which are adjustable.

A wheel-frame is provided at the lower part of the machine,
and by running the machine down hill whilst actuating suitable
treadles the machine is caused to rise by reason of the flapping motion of the wings.

Several pairs of wings may be employed in one machine,
and steam or other power may be employed instead of manual
power.

(*Drawings.*)

A.D. 1884.   No. 15023.

BOULT, Alfred Julius.   (*Communicated by Alphonse Aubrée.*)

" NAVIGABLE BALLOON."

Two pear-shaped balloons are connected together by a car

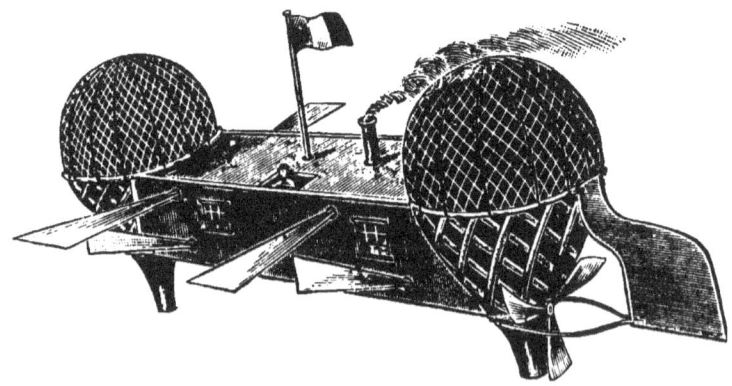

containing the motive power, and the propelling is performed
by oars and a screw.

A rudder is employed for steering.

A.D. 1885. No. 1549.

LAKE, William Robert. (*Communicated by Eugene F. Falconnet.*)

"NAVIGABLE BALLOON."

THE "frame, gas-field, hull, and cabin" of an elongated cylindrical air-vessel is constructed of one general frame of metal jointed and braced together. Cross-girders, bulk-heads, posts, and braces are employed in the construction of the frame.

The buoyancy of the air-ship is regulated by means of an air-sack situated in the gas-holder, and the vessel is covered with a roof provided with gutters and spouts, to protect it from the elements.

"Wheel-houses" carry the propelling-screws, and a vertical screw regulates the altitude of the machine. Fin-shaped rudders are used for steering, and adjustable fans are employed as sails when the wind is fair.

This complicated specification has 71 claims, and the drawings contain 85 figures.

(*Drawings.*)

A.D. 1885. No. 4618.

CLARK, Alexander Melville. (*Communicated by Moses Liberia Stilwell Buckner.*)

"WAR BALLOONS."

EXPLOSIVES are suspended to a frame attached to a balloon, and clock-work or other means is provided for releasing the explosives at a predetermined time.

The balloon may be allowed to drift, or be propelled over the hostile force, when the explosives are released as above stated.

(*Drawing.*)

A.D. 1885.   No. 5118.

HENDERSON, Arthur Charles. (*Communicated by Blaise*
B. Bontems.)

"NAVIGABLE BALLOONS."

WINGS are attached to a frame situated between a balloon
and its car, the said wings being worked by a hand-lever.

The motions of the wings are intended to imitate those of
birds, and auxiliary mechanical birds may be actuated at the
sides of the car.

(*Drawings.*)

A.D. 1885.   No. 5854.

BRUCE, Eric Stuart.

"BALLOON SIGNALLING."

ONE or more incandescence lamps are suspended within a

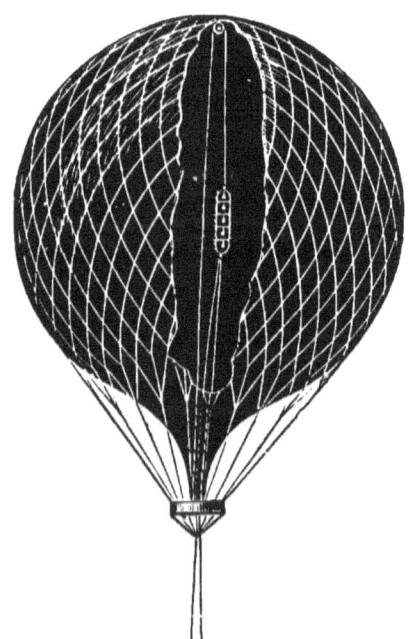

balloon, and an electric current is supplied to the lamps by a conductor on the captive rope. By alternately breaking and connecting the circuit the balloon is illuminated by flashes of any required duration, or the balloon may be illuminated continuously.

A.D. 1885. No. 7727.

BATE, Henry.

"Balloon Railway."

Elongated balloons are employed with a travelling endless rope in a balloon railway.

(*Drawing.*)

A.D. 1885. No. 8567.

HUTCHINSON, William Nelson.

"Testing Screw Propellers."

A machine is described for gauging the push of screw propellers intended for aërial propulsion.

The screw to be tested is mounted on a horizontal shaft, which shaft is provided at its end with a spring indicator.

(*Drawing.*)

A.D. 1885. No. 9193.

OWEN, Richard George.

"Flying Machine."

A framework is provided with a seat, and two propellers, mounted on vertical axes at the upper part of the framework, are rotated by treadles actuated by the person riding the machine.

A.D. 1885.   No. 9472.

AUSTIN, Charles Edward, and BURCHELL, William.

" PROPELLING BALLOONS."

A CASING or tube is attached longitudinally to an elongated balloon, and within the tube a sheet of pliable elastic material is placed, and receives a reciprocal movement. In this manner the air is drawn in at one end of the tube and forced out at the other, thus propelling the balloon.

(*Drawing.*)

A.D. 1885.   No. 9585.

PRESTWICH, William Henry.

" NAVIGABLE BALLOONS."

AN elongated balloon is propelled by means of a pair of feathering paddles, which are similar in construction to those described in specification No. 11994, A.D. 1884.

By attaching the balloon out of centre to a horizontal bar forming the frame below the balloon, gyration is avoided.

The direction of the paddles may be changed for the purpose of steering, and a rudder is employed for the same purpose.

"Lappets," or parachute-like wings, are attached to the sides of the balloon to prevent a rapid descent in case of accident.

(*Drawings.*)

A.D. 1885.   No. 11158.

WINKLER, August.

"NAVIGABLE BALLOON."

A BALLOON is propelled by the action of escaping jets of fluid, which exhaust the air in front of an umbrella-like surface. This surface, which is attached to the car, is drawn forward towards the vacuum, and the balloon may be steered by altering the direction of this propelling-apparatus.

(*Drawing.*)

A.D. 1885.   No. 14827.

LAKE, William Robert.   (*Communicated by Eugene F. Falconnet.*)

"NAVIGABLE BALLOONS."

THIS specification describes the construction of elongated navigable balloons, in which a metal frame is employed within the aërostat.   The balloons are propelled and steered by screws, and the interiors of the balloons are subdivided into several gas-tight compartments.

(*Drawings.*)

108

A.D. 1885.   No. 15627.

ARCHIBALD, Edmund Douglas.

"KITE-BALLOON."

A KITE is employed in combination with a captive balloon,

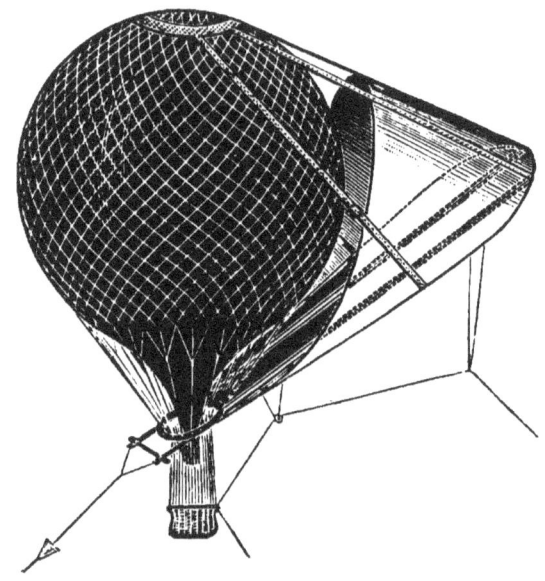

whereby ascents may suitably be made in windy weather.

A.D. 1886.   No. 1821.

YBARGOITIA, Felipe Modet é.

"BALLOON RAILWAY."

A BALLOON is attached to a pair of wheels running between two pairs of rails, situated on the ground or anchored in water.

The rope is connected to a winch in the car of the balloon, and springs are employed on the rope to prevent jars of the balloon being communicated to the rails.

(*Drawings.*)

A.D. 1886.   No. 1830.

WAELDE, Jacob.
"FLYING MACHINE."

A FLYING machine is propelled by a pair of revolving frames, which carry feathering paddles. A rudder is employed for steering, and the machine may be actuated by an electric motor, the electric current being supplied from a stationary dynamo-electric machine on the ground.

(*Drawing.*)

A.D. 1886.   No. 7015.

REDFERN, George Frederick. (*Communicated by Joseph Symonds Foster.*)
"FLYING MACHINE."

A SEAT is attached to a frame carrying a wheel, pedals, and two vertical screw propellers. The aëronaut rotates the propellers by means of the pedals, and thus causes the machine to fly.

(*Drawing.*)

A.D. 1886.   No. 7837.

MOLESWORTH-HEPWORTH, Edward Newall.
"NAVIGABLE BALLOON."

A LONGITUDINAL spar is suspended by a net to an elongated balloon, which latter may be subdivided or composed of a number of small balloons enclosed in an outer envelope.

The car is suspended by rods which hang fulcrumed to the centre of the longitudinal spar, and by means of cords, which connect the car to the extremities of the spar, the said car can be adjusted in position and so change the horizontal position of the balloon. An aëroplane is attached to the spar, and the balloon is propelled by a propeller actuated by the feet of the passenger. Air is pumped into an elastic reservoir situated in the balloon, or allowed to escape in order to keep a uniform tension.

(*Drawing.*)

A.D. 1886.   No. 8051.

HUTCHINSON, William Nelson.

"NAVIGABLE BALLOONS."

ELONGATED balloons are provided with a tube or bar running the full length of the balloon and along the lower surface. By means of weights and springs this tube or bar is employed to compress the balloon for the purpose of keeping the surface smooth or to cause a rapid descent.

(*Drawing.*)

A.D. 1886.   No. 9452.

CLARK, Alexander Melville.   (*Communicated by Amédée Mathurin Gabriel Sebillot.*)

"NAVIGABLE BALLOON."

AN elongated balloon is built of metal, and is propelled by a screw, which is actuated by a steam-motor.   The heat from the smoke-stacks of the steam-generators is fed into the balloon for the purpose of dilating the air within the balloon, and thus dispensing with hydrogen or other gas.

The balloon is constructed with an inner frame of nickel-plated steel, covered with a strong envelope composed of two sheets of asbestos with wire netting between.   The balloon may be divided into compartments, each of which may be kept at any required temperature.

(*Drawings.*)

111

A.D. 1886. No. 13901.

LEMMON, Sydney.

"AËRIAL MACHINE."

AN aërial machine is described which may be also operated on land or water. It is supported in the air by "balloons or air-vessels," and propelled by paddles worked by foot-power.

Shells may be dropped on the enemy, when an extra balloon would be attached to support the weight of the shell.

(*Drawing.*)

A.D. 1887. No. 316.

HADDAN, Herbert John. (*Communicated by Arthur de Bausset.*)

"NAVIGABLE BALLOON."

AN elongated balloon of cylindrical form with pointed ends is constructed of solid steel plates, and is preferably about 414 feet long. The lifting power is obtained by producing a vacuum in the balloon, and the propulsion is obtained by

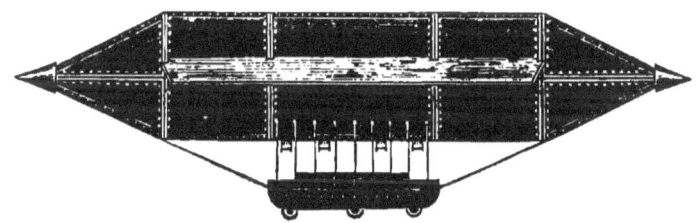

ejecting air against the atmosphere. Aëroplanes are provided on either side, and the car is suspended in such a manner that it may be adjusted longitudinally below the balloon.

A.D. 1887. No. 5644.

HUTCHINSON, William Nelson.

"PROPELLING BALLOONS."

A ROTARY·blowing-engine is employed to project a jet of air from a nozzle for the purpose of propelling balloons.

By adjusting the jet the balloon may be steered in any direction.

(*Drawing.*)

A.D. 1887. No. 8182.

JOHNSON, James Yate. (*Communicated by Alexandre Ciurcu.*)

" JET PROPULSION."

A COMPOUND consisting of nitrate of ammonia, petroleum, and charcoal is burnt within a closed vessel, contained in the car of the balloon. The gas formed by this combustion is permitted to escape through a suitable orifice, and thus propel the balloon in a contrary direction to the escape of the jet.

(*Drawing.*)

A.D. 1887. No. 8255.

GUSTAFSON, Wald.

" NAVIGABLE BALLOON."

AN elongated balloon supports a framework carrying a pro-

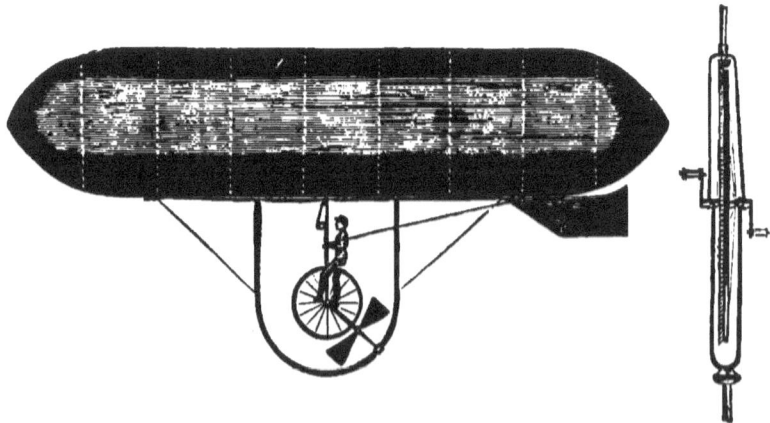

peller which is actuated by the aëronaut. The propeller may

be adjusted in position in order to propel or regulate the altitude of the balloon.

Other power may be employed, and any number of persons may assist in propelling the balloon.

A.D. 1887.   No. 8386.

RIBEIRO, Joaquim Ignacio.

"Navigable Balloon."

Two pairs of paddles actuated by the aëronaut are employed for propelling an elongated balloon, the paddles being set at right angles to each other and made to alternately feather and hold the air. This action may be adjusted so that they tend to propel the balloon up or down, or backwards or forwards.

Two side aëroplanes, a tail, and a number of louvre flaps are employed to steady the balloon, and the side aëroplanes may be folded like fans.

An adjustable weight is employed for trimming the balloon. (*Drawing.*)

A.D. 1887.   No. 9665.

NORMAN, John James.

" Inflating Fire-Balloons."

LIQUID or gaseous fuel is fed, under pressure, to burners situated within a hood ; it is then burnt, and the products of combustion are fed through a pipe having a flexible joint to the interior of a balloon.

The burner can also be suspended to the mouth of the balloon, and be employed during ascents, when a curtain is employed to confine the ascending heat. (*Drawing.*)

A.D. 1887.   **No. 11941.**

THOMPSON, William Phillips.   (*Communicated by George C. Baker.*)

" PROPELLING AND REGULATING."

A PROPELLER is mounted on an adjustable arm in such a manner that it may be caused to act in any direction.

The propeller is rotated from a main driving-shaft by means of bevel gearing.

(*Drawing.*)

A.D. 1887.   **No. 15567.**

LANE, Howard.

" MAKING BALLOONS."

MATERIAL for making balloons is shaped to the desired form by means of a spindle having tapering extremities.   The

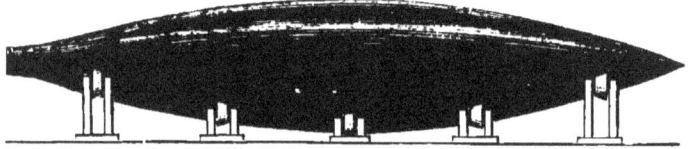

spindle is supported on anti-friction wheels, and the material is spread on the spindle whilst it is being rotated.

A.D. 1888.   **No. 508.**

PARKINSON, George Seaborn.

" NAVIGABLE BALLOON."

AN elongated balloon is propelled by the reaction of three jets of air, which are ejected from trumpet-shaped mouths situated at the stern and on either side of the balloon.

The air is forced through the mouths by means of a fan

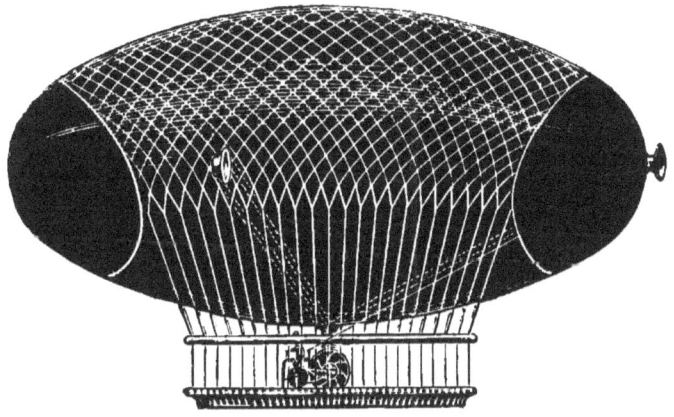

or blower, which is actuated by the aëronaut or by a suitable motor.

A.D. 1888.   No. 4552.

APRAXIN, Count Anton.

"BALLOON RAILWAY."

AN endless rope passes round pulleys situated on either side of a ravine or river, and the rope is made to travel by actuating the pulleys. Two or more balloons are attached to the rope by rigid rods, and the balloons support the weight to be transported.

(*Drawing.*)

A.D. 1888.   No. 5742.

GAGGINO, Giovanni.

" NAVIGABLE BALLOONS."

THE ascending or descending force of an elongated balloon is employed to cause it to ascend or descend forward on an inclined plane.

An aëroplane is attached to the zone of the balloon, and rudders are provided for steering horizontally or vertically.

A balance-weight is suspended below the balloon to regulate the angle of its inclination.

(*Drawing.*)

A.D. 1888.   No. 9448.

BEUGGER, John.

"Navigable Balloon."

THE balloon has preferably the shape of a biconvex lens, and is distended by an internal frame composed of ⋂-shaped rods.

The car carries two propellers, which are actuated by two motors, and by driving the propellers at varying speeds the balloon may be guided to the right or left, or the steering may be performed by a rudder.

The vertical direction of the balloon is regulated by an adjustable weight, or by increasing or decreasing the speed of the propellers.

The lifting-power of the balloon alone is not sufficient to cause an ascent, so that it is only when the propellers force the machine ahead, causing the balloon to act as an aëroplane, that flight can be accomplished.

A.D. 1888.   **No. 9725.**

MIDDLETON, Henry.

" FLYING MACHINE."

A PAIR of wings, which are preferably concave on their under surface, are flapped up and down by the piston of a cylinder which is actuated by steam or other power.

The wings are composed of elastic ribs attached to a main rod, which latter is fulcrumed to a link attached to the cylinder, and its inner end is connected to the end of the piston-rod.

The wings are made to turn on the rods in order to feather in the air.

Modifications are shown, but the construction of all the details is not fully described.

(*Drawings.*)

A.D. 1888.   **No. 10937.**

FARINI, Guillermo Antonio, and BALDWIN, Thomas Scott.

" PARACHUTE."

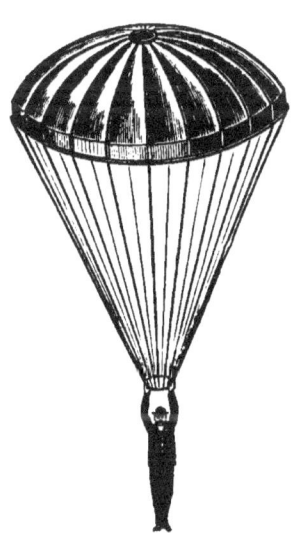

A FLEXIBLE parachute is made mushroom-shaped with a hole at the top for the passage of air.

Cords are sewn on the seams, and a cord is also sewn round the lower edge of the parachute.

A.D. 1888.   **No. 11354.**

LORRAIN, James Grieve.

"ELECTRICAL PROPULSION."

ELECTRO-STATIC motors, which influence machines of the "Wimshurst" type, are employed for propelling aërial vessels, and the electricity is supplied from a primary battery consisting of a large number of small cells.

In cases where the electro-motor is on a captive balloon, the current may be conveyed from apparatus on the earth.

A screw which is employed for propelling may also steer the machine.

(*Drawing.*)

A.D. 1888.   **No. 12736.**

HILFREICH, Francis.

"NAVIGABLE BALLOON."

THIS specification describes a balloon which is substantially identical with the one described in specification No. 11994 A.D. 1884, by the same inventor.

Screw propellers are mounted at the front of the cars to facilitate ascending and descending.

(*Drawing.*)

A.D. 1888.   **No. 14610.**

MONTEITH, Joseph.

"BALLOON RAILWAY."

ELONGATED balloons are provided with an electric motor for actuating screws for propelling and regulating the altitude.

Electricity is supplied from a carriage running on an insulated railway-track, the current passing through the rails.

Several arrangements of propellers and balloons are shown.

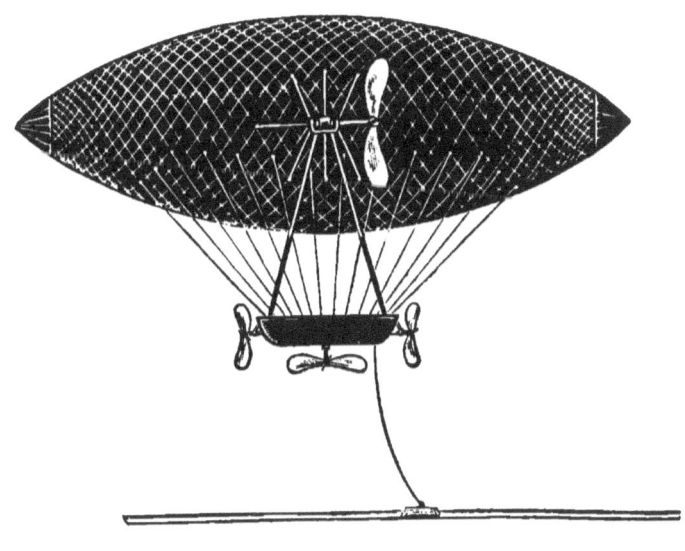

A.D. 1889.

No. 47.

WORMS, James.

" Navigable Balloon."

An aëroplane is attached to the underside of an elongated

balloon, the connecting-cords being continued down to support the car. A motor is provided in the car for actuating a pair of wings, and a weight is adjusted below the aëroplane to regulate the angle of the balloon.

The ascent is effected by working the wings, and a forward motion is obtained by placing the weight in front of the apparatus, thus causing the descent to be made on an inclined plane.

By moving the weight to one side the machine may be steered horizontally.

A.D. 1889.　　　　　　　　　　　　　　　　No. 1671.

EDWARDS, Edmund. (*Communicated by Jean Joseph Gloton.*)

"NAVIGABLE BALLOON."

AN elongated balloon of the form of a haystack is constructed of metal plates rivetted and soldered together.

Vertical screws are employed for regulating the altitude, and a horizontal screw is mounted at the stern for propelling. Two rudders are pivotted in the stern for steering purposes.

(*Drawing.*)

A.D. 1889.　　　　　　　　　　　　　　　　No. 3360.

CRAIG, John.

"FLYING MACHINE."

A FRAMEWORK of wood or of metal tubing is covered with cloth; above this framework two propellers are mounted on vertical axes, and naphtha turbines are mounted below the frame for driving the propellers.

No mechanism is provided for horizontal propulsion, though a rudder is shown for steering the machine.

(*Drawing.*)

A.D. 1889.

No. 3957.

BASTARD, William John.

" NAVIGABLE BALLOON.

THE balloon, which is elongated in form, is contained in a frame consisting of upper and lower longitudinal rods and circumferential ribs. The interior of the balloon is subdivided, and an elastic pocket is provided below for the reception of the overflow gas.

Two propellers are mounted on either side for propelling the balloon, and these propellers are actuated by the aëronauts, and may be partly worked by wind-fans mounted at the top of the balloon.

Rudders are mounted at the bow and stern for steering purposes, and a line connects these two rudders in such a manner that they may be actuated simultaneously.

(*Drawing.*)

A.D. 1889.

No. 4301.

DALE, William Duncombe.

"BALLOON PARACHUTE."

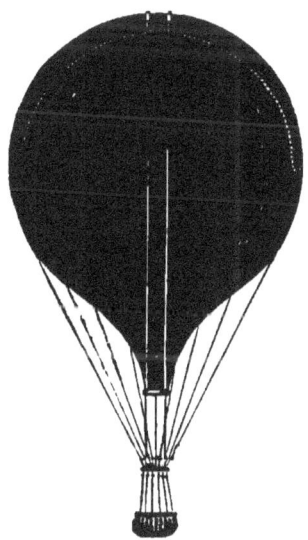

VALVES are fitted at the neck and at the top of a balloon.

Two guide-cords descend through the balloon from the top valve to the ring, and the lower valve is free to travel on these guide-cords. The upper valve is constructed of netting, covered with gas-proof material, and by pulling the above-mentioned material away the gas escapes, and the force of air caused by the rapid descent causes the lower part of the balloon to rise inside the upper part, and thus form a parachute.

A.D. 1889.   No. 4811.

RIECKERT, Herman August Julius, and RIECKERT, Albert Emil Karl.

" NAVIGABLE BALLOON."

AN elongated balloon is composed of three compartments, situated one above the other, the lower compartment being strengthened by a strong wooden framework. The second compartment is attached to the upper surface of the lower one, and the third compartment is situated above the second and shifts its position according to the direction of the wind.

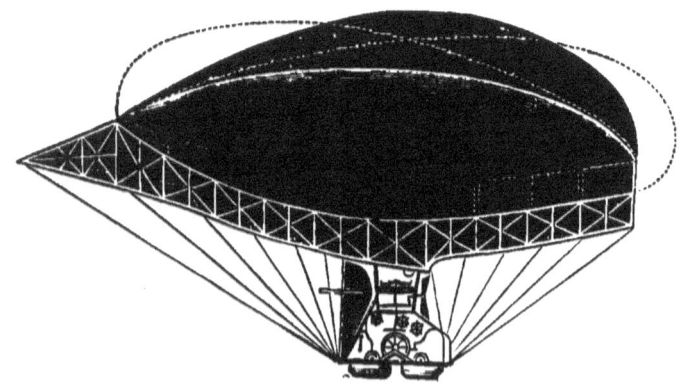

A fan or propeller is driven by treadle mechanism, and the passengers are provided with seats within a closed car. Four boats are carried below the car for supporting the apparatus should a descent be made on water.

A.D. 1889. No. 6419.

CHAMBERS, Jesse Mary.

" PROPELLING BALLOONS."

BALLOONS are to be propelled by the reaction of jets of air which are forced by means of two pairs of bellows attached to the sides of the car.

The sides of the bellows may act as wings, and by adjusting the said bellows the balloon may be propelled in any direction.

(*Drawing.*)

A.D. 1889. No. 7427.

ZIMER, Frederick William.

" NAVIGABLE BALLOON."

AN elongated balloon having a concave under surface is propelled by a screw propeller actuated by treadle mechanism.

The underside of the balloon is made rigid by means of metal tubing, and the upper part of the balloon is kept to the required shape by thin bands of steel ribbon. The fabric of the balloon is held down onto the frame by means of cords, and by loosening these cords the fabric forms a parachute.

The car, which is elongated and very deep, is mounted on a keel attached to the underside of the balloon, on which keel it is free to slide, the centre of gravity of the balloon being thus adjusted.

. The propeller-blades are composed of tubular framework covered with canvas, and the steering is effected by means of rudders.

A.D. 1889.   No. 11108.

ROBINSON, George.
" AËRIAL MACHINE."

A RECTANGULAR box has gas-bags attached to two of its sides and "hinged elevators" attached to its ends.

A gas-engine in the box rotates two shafts having screw propellers at both ends.

This specification is very vague, the utility of several parts not being described.

(*Drawing.*)

A.D. 1889.   No. 12320.

THAYER, David.
" KITES."

A NUMBER of kites, with or without balloons attached at the rear of same, are employed for elevating passengers, &c., in the air, and also for towing vessels over land or water. Controlling lines are connected to the sides of the kites in order to control the direction of the kites as may be required.

By connecting a balloon to the upper part of a kite the failure of wind will not cause it to descend.

(*Drawings.*)

A.D. 1889.   No. 13207.

DAVIDSON, George Louis Outram.
" AËRIAL MACHINE."

AN elongated balloon is attached above a ' body surface," to which latter the car is attached, and to which two wings and bow and stern rudders are pivotted.

The "power of the attraction of the earth" is employed as a means of propulsion.

(*Drawings.*)

A.D. 1889.   No. 14737.

OTTO, Edward Charles Frederick, and OTTO, Edward Charles Frederick (Junior).

" NAVIGATING BALLOONS AND FLYING MACHINES."

BALLOONS and flying machines are to be propelled and sustained, partially or wholly so, by three distinct arrangements of mechanism.

1. By employing feathering paddles, which are made to revolve and only hold the air on one quarter of their revolution. The paddles, of which there are four in each set, are constructed on the principle described in the abridgement of No. 11994, A.D. 1884, and by rotating the sets of paddles at varying speeds the direction of the balloon may be varied.

Mr. Otto, who is the inventor of the bicycle which bears his name, seems to have embodied some of the details of his bicycle invention in this specification on aëronautics.

2. The second arrangement describes a pair of wings which are actuated by the direct action of a piston-rod, the said wings cleaving the air when moving upwards and forwards, and employing their full acting surface in the downward motion.

3. The third propelling arrangement consists of a chamber having its rear end open to the atmosphere, through which opening periodical sudden discharges of steam are forced.

The car is adjustable longitudinally below the balloon, and side aëroplanes are employed either with or without a balloon.

(*Drawings.*)

A.D. 1889.   No. 16883.

MAXIM, Hiram Stevens.

"FLYING MACHINE."

THE object of this invention is to construct a flying machine having great power, effectually expended ; and every part of the machine is constructed as lightly as possible, consistent with the necessary strength.

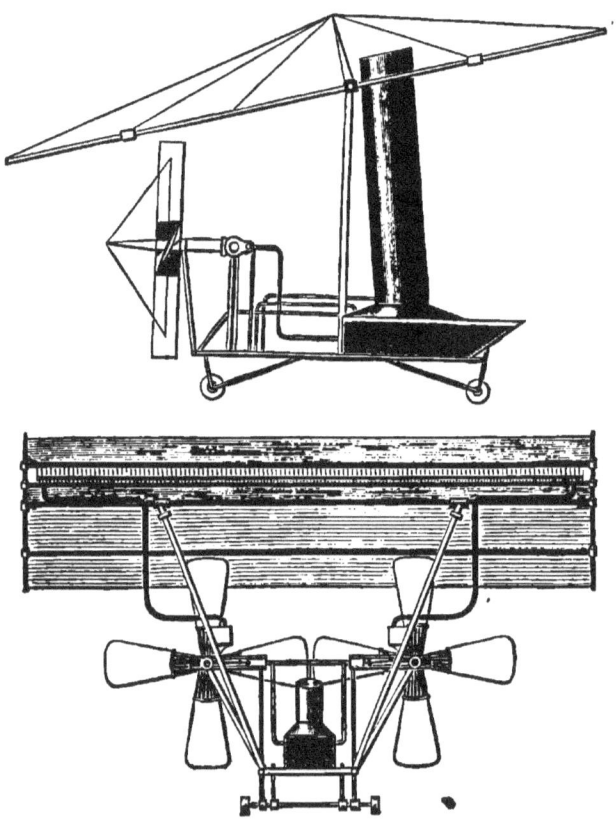

An aëroplane, composed of tubes covered with fabric, is pivotted to the main frame in such a manner that it may be adjusted, up or down, to any required angle.

Two propellers, constructed of spokes covered with silk, are mounted side by side on the frame below the aëroplane, and by driving these propellers at varying speeds the machine may be steered to the right or left.

The propellers are driven by separate engines, supplied with steam from a boiler composed of comparatively large tubes connected together by tubes of very small diameter, thus giving a large heating surface; and the heating of such boiler is effected by the combustion of vaporized hydrocarbon.

A condenser, composed of flat tubes, is situated in the aëroplane, or the aëroplane may act as a condenser itself if constructed of two skins; thus the necessity of carrying a large quantity of water for the boiler is obviated, as by means of the condenser the water may be used over and over again.

The speed of the engines may be regulated by barometric means, thus enabling the machine to be kept at any required altitude, as by increasing the speed of the propellers the machine will rise, and by decreasing the speed the machine will descend.

The machine is started on rails, one pair of rails being below the wheels and another pair a short distance above them. By running the machine along, it can be noticed whether the wheels run in contact with the upper or the lower pair of rails, and the required inclination of the aëroplane may thus be ascertained before the apparatus rises in the air.

A modification of the invention is described, in which the aëroplane is fixed to the main frame, and auxiliary aëroplanes are pivotted at the bow and stern for the purpose of steering the apparatus vertically.

The framework of the machine is built of steel tubes, trussed together, with the object of gaining the greatest amount of strength with the smallest expenditure of weight.

There are 35 claims and 12 sheets of drawings to this specification.

A.D. 1889.   No. 18952.

HOWSON, William.

"War Balloons."

Balloons are employed for conveying and automatically discharging shells of either illuminating, asphyxiating, or explosive capacity. The shells on being discharged allow of an escape of gas from the balloon by actuating a valve by means of a connecting-cord.

A telescopic valve is described, as well as various constructions of shells and means for discharging same.

Shells may be conveyed on the captive rope of a balloon by means of auxiliary balloons, and torpedoes may be employed in conjunction with balloons.

Various warlike manœuvres are described.

(*Drawings.*)

A.D. 1889. No. 19209.

TIELKE-ALLAN, Francis Henrick.

" NAVIGABLE BALLOON."

THIS inventor has adopted the plan described in specification No. 2154, A.D. 1856, in which the balloon is provided with a helical worm or blades, and by rotating the balloon it forms its own propeller.

In the particular arrangement described, two horizontal balloons are mounted on a shaft, and the car is suspended from the centre of the shaft between the balloons. The balloons are rotated by gearing from the car, and they may be subdivided into compartments.

(*Drawing.*)

A.D. 1890. No. 4647.

RADOTINSKY, Josef.

" BALLOON."

BALLOONS are made in two chambers, the upper one, which is in the shape of an inverted heart, being made of the ordinary fabric, and the lower chamber being constructed of aluminium, so as to form a rigid case. By pumping gas from the upper chamber into the lower one, the balloon is caused to descend, whilst by allowing gas to return to the upper chamber an ascent is effected. A cord which is attached

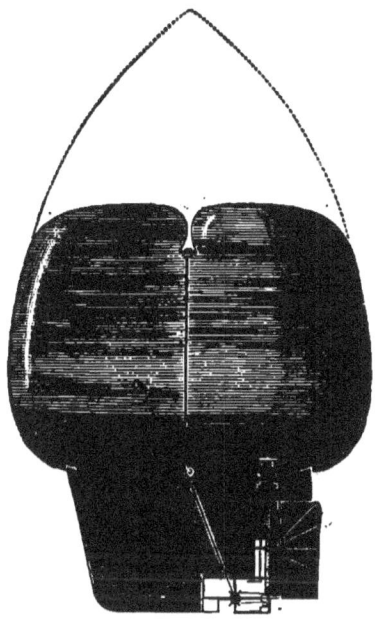

to the upper part of the balloon is drawn down when the gas is being withdrawn, for the purpose of preventing damage being caused to the balloon whilst making the descent.

A rudder is provided for steering, and a propeller is also shown, though no particular means for actuating same is described.

A.D. 1890. No. 5404.

GREY, Ernest Howard.

"NAVIGABLE BALLOON."

THE balloon is constructed of a framework of wire or bamboo, covered with silk, and the interior is divided into separate compartments.

K

A frame which is attached to the balloon carries a saddle,

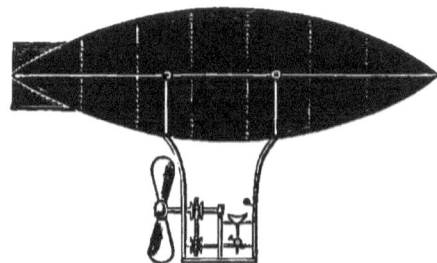

treadle mechanism, and a propeller, and the aëronaut is thus enabled to propel the balloon.

A.D. 1890.   No. 8816.

HARRIS, Henry Marmaduke.

"Aërial Machine."

This machine is built in the shape of a boat, and compartments are provided at the bow and stern for containing gas.

A blast is blown through a funnel, which being adjustable enables the vessel to be steered. A balloon is fastened to the vessel to assist and control the ascent and descent.

(*Drawing*.)

A D. 1890.   No. 11455.

CAIRNCROSS, Stewart.

" Navigable Balloon."

A RECTANGULAR framework covered with a light glazed material forms the lower part of a balloon ; and at the centre of this frame two pendulum arms are fulcrumed, at the lower ends of which arms a car is attached.

A propeller is mounted on a horizontal shaft situated on the frame below the balloon, the said shaft being actuated by the aëronaut through gearing communicating with treadle and hand mechanism in the car. A rope is fastened to the bow of the frame and thence over a pulley in the car to the stern of the frame. By rotating the pulley, the car is adjusted in

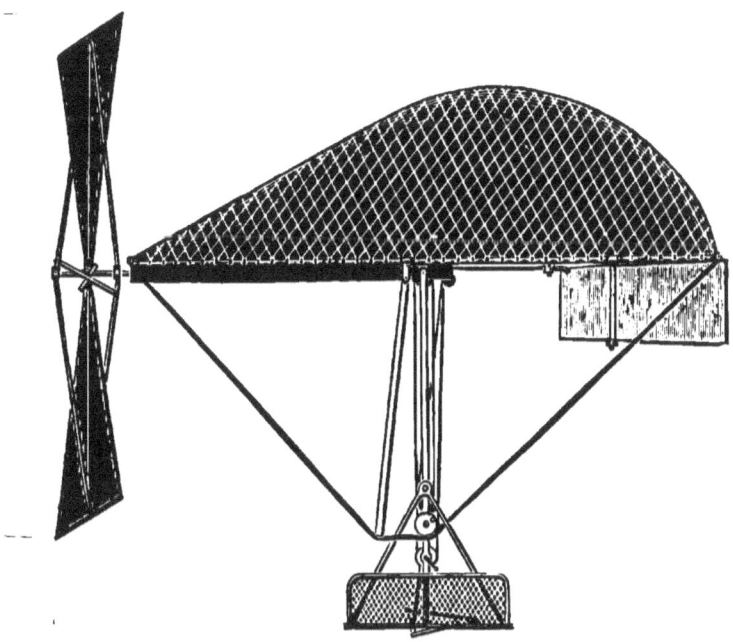

position below the balloon, and thus enables the balloon and propeller to be regulated in position up or down.

A.D. 1890.　　　　　　　　　　　　　　No. 12349.

GRIFFITHS, Thomas, and BEDDOES, Thomas Henry Willoughby.

"JET PROPULSION."

GASES or explosives are ignited within a tube, where they expand, and in escaping against the outer atmosphere cause the propulsion of the aëronautic machine to which the apparatus is attached.

(*Drawing.*)

A.D. 1890.   No. 13099.

HUELSER, Charles.   (*Communicated by Sophus Hartmann and Max Nathan.*)

"NAVIGABLE BALLOON."

An elongated balloon is provided with a longitudinal framework, on each side of which are mounted frames carrying valve flaps. These frames are reciprocated backwards and forwards, the valve flaps closing and opening alternately, thus propelling the balloon.

(*Drawing.*)

A.D. 1890.   No. 13311.

MOORE, Ross Franklin.

"FLYING MACHINE."

This machine is constructed in imitation of a bat, with a frame below for carrying the driving-power and the load. The wings, which are made of a bamboo, steel, or aluminium frame covered with gold-beater's skin, silk, or light cloth, are made to oscillate, and are given a rocking motion.

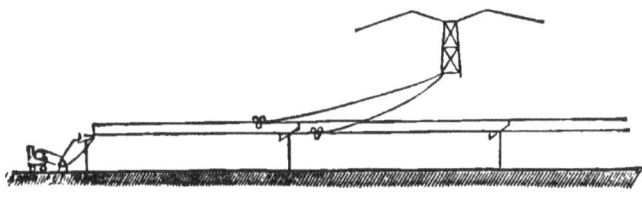

The machine can receive an electric current from lines on the ground, and thus dispense with the weight of batteries.

The drawings accompanying this specification are simply diagrammatic views.

A.D. 1890.   No. 15332

BOULT, Alfred Julius.   (*Communicated by Wilhelm Ellingen.*)

"BALLOON RAILWAY."

A CABLE is placed loosely on the ground between two points where a balloon is required to travel, and the cable is passed

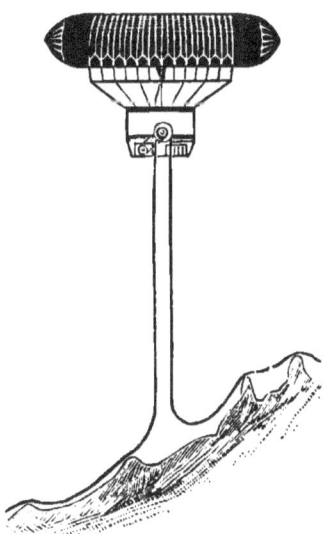

over a pulley situated in the car of the balloon.   The pulley is rotated by an electro-motor in the car and thus draws the balloon along in the direction of the rope.

A.D. 1890.   No. 15850.

WELLS, Clara Louisa.

"BALLOON RAILWAY."

BALLOONS are connected to a ring running on a line, which ring is drawn from place to place by ropes actuated by a stationary engine.

The description is most vague, and suggestions are made for its application to travelling by land or sea, and also for training of birds to aid the balloons.

(*Drawings.*)

A.D. 1890.   No. 20435.

PHILLIPS, Horatio Frederick.

"FLYING MACHINE."

THIS invention is based upon a previous invention, No. 13768, A.D. 1884, by the same inventor, in which he described the use of blades having convex upper surfaces. By giving these blades a rapid forward motion, a partial vacuum is formed above, thereby giving them a lifting power.

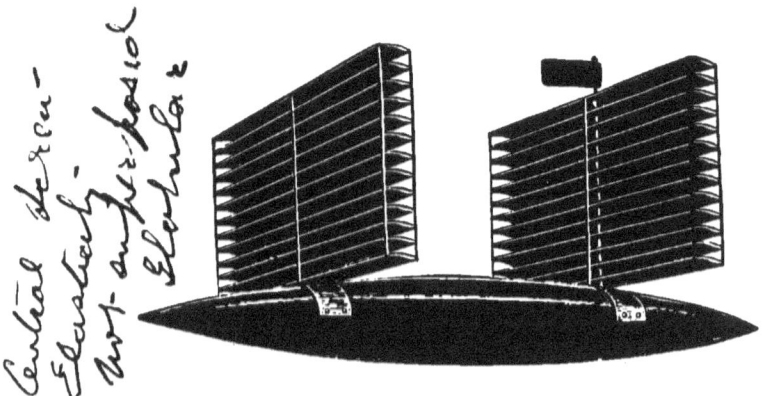

According to this present invention a number of these blades are placed one above the other in a frame, and two or more of these frames are attached to the upper part of a body which is propelled by apparatus not described or shown.

A.D. 1890.   No. 21241.

HUTCHINSON, William Nelson.

"BALLOONS."

SALMON-SHAPED balloons are to have their upper halves constructed of thin metal, with a ridge running along the centre to throw off snow.

A.D. 1891. ‾   No. 1555.

SINCLAIR, William Houston.

" NAVIGABLE BALLOON."

AN elongated balloon is constructed of bamboo-canes covered with air-proof fabric. A pair of paddles, actuated by any suitable power, are employed for propelling, and the feathering blades of such paddles may be on light tubular-steel frames acting as venetians covered with strong silk. " The lowest deck is 96 feet long, and the balloon is divided into three parts."

(Drawings.)

A.D. 1891.   No. 1943.

HUTCHINSON, William Nelson.

" BALLOONS."

BALLOONS of various forms are made of sheet metal, strengthened internally by struts abutting against ribs attached to the interior.

Air is withdrawn through holes in the lower part of the balloon, and hydrogen is admitted at the upper part, the interior openings of these outlets and inlets being protected by discs, to prevent the air mixing with the hydrogen through agitation.

A.D. 1891.   No. 4090.

MUNNS, William Henry. *(Communicated by William Willshire Riley.)*

" APPLICATION OF BALLOON."

A BALLOON is attached to the top of a tubular mast of a boat, and gas is supplied to the balloon from compressed gas reservoirs in the boat.

The balloon keeps the boat afloat in case of it becoming filled with water, and it also acts as a sail to attract the attention of passing ships.

(Drawings.)

A.D. 1891.   No. 4485.

NAHL, Perham Wilhelm.

"NAVIGABLE BALLOON."

AN elongated balloon, constructed in separate compartments, is provided with an aëroplane on either side, which increase in width towards the stern. Two propellers, one on either side of the balloon, are actuated by electric motors, which are supplied with electricity from secondary batteries. The propellers with their motors are mounted on a shaft, which

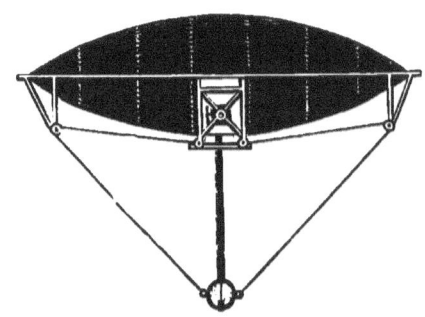

enables their position to be adjusted by means of a hand wheel. A rod which is fulcrumed below the balloon carries a hollow ball at its lower end containing sand, and by adjusting this rod forward or backward the angle of the balloon may be adjusted. By opening a valve at the lower part of the ball, sand may be discharged from same and thus serve the purpose of ballast.

———————

A.D. 1891.   No. 8142.

BOULT, Alfred Julius. (*Communicated by Arthur de Bausset.*)

"NAVIGABLE BALLOON."

AN elongated metal balloon is given the necessary ascentional force by creating a more or less complete vacuum within same. The balloon, which is constructed of thin steel plates, is strengthened by an internal framework, and the inventor considers 738 ft. long and 144 ft. diameter to be suitable dimensions.

Aëroplanes, inclined downwards at an angle of about 45°, project from either side of the balloon.

A car is suspended below the balloon and is adjustable longitudinally, thus regulating the angle of the apparatus.

An exhaust fan is employed to propel the machine by the impact of a current of air, and by adjusting the outlet the direction of propulsion may be controlled at will.

This invention is very similar to No. 316, A.D. 1887, by the same inventor.

(*Drawings.*)

A.D. 1891.   No. 11212.

NEWTON, Alfred Vincent. (*Communicated by Alfred Nobel.*)

"MOTIVE POWER."

A LIGHT motive power is obtained by the decomposition of water or other liquid within a closed vessel, through the action thereon of metallic sodium, potassium, finely-divided manganese or other metals having a like affinity for oxygen. The hydrogen which escapes is employed to work an engine for driving a balloon, or a jet in escaping into the atmosphere may be employed for direct propulsion by means of its repulsive power.

(*Drawing.*)

A.D. 1891.   No. 12403.

FYERS, William Augustus.

"BALLOON."

A BALLOON is made in the form of a ring so that it will not obstruct the car in the event of a descent at sea. The car, which may be covered with waterproof canvas, is suspended close up to the balloon, and by dividing the said balloon into separate compartments the danger from bullets in time of war is obviated.

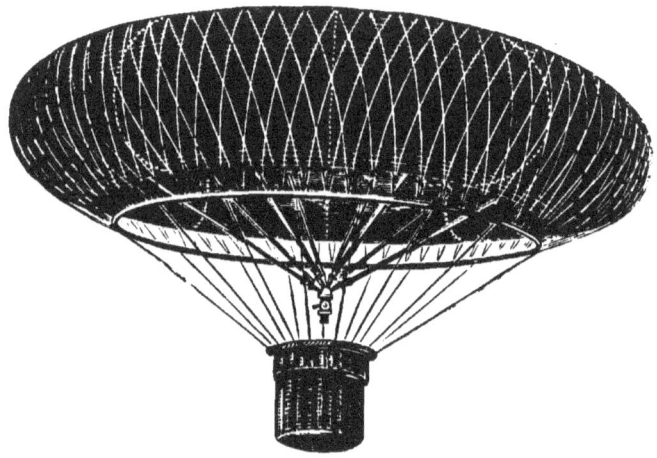

A second car may be suspended below the above mentioned car.

A.D. 1891. No. 12669.

EDWARDS, Edmund. (*Communicated by Ludwig Rohrmann.*)

" BIRDS-EYE PHOTOGRAPHY."

A ROCKET or projectile, containing a camera attached to a parachute, is projected over the place to be photographed.

On arriving over the desired spot the rocket or projectile

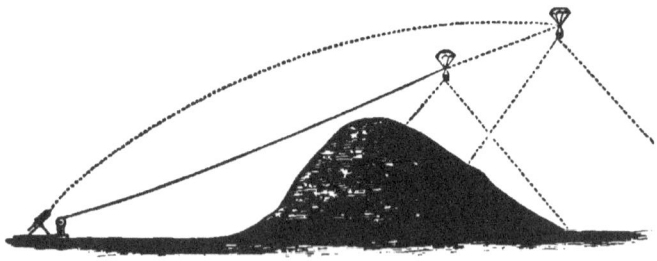

explodes, thereby liberating the camera and parachute, which may be drawn back by a cord after the exposure of the negative.

PHILLIPS, Horatio Frederick.

" FLYING MACHINES."

BLADES or sustainers (*i. e.* aëroplanes) are made with a
convex upper surface, and a lower surface concave in front

and convex towards the rear end. The convex underpart
prevents the formation of an eddy below the front portion of
the aëroplane.

A.D. 1891.   No. 14742.

MOY, Thomas.

" GOVERNING AËRIAL MACHINES."

Two appliances are described for governing aërial machines,
the movement of which is regulated by the action of a
pendulum.

In the first apparatus, two idle toothed wheels are rotated
by contact with right and left screws, situated on a sleeve
sliding on a rectangular shaft. The two toothed wheels are
mounted in sliding bearings which are pressed towards each
other by springs ; and a pendulum having a cross arm at its
upper part is suspended from a point between the wheels.
On the pendulum swinging, one end of the cross arm takes
into one of the toothed wheels and clamps it, thus throwing
it out of gear with the other wheel. The sleeve now moves
along the rectangular shaft, taking with it a lever which
actuates a plane or rudder, thus correcting the angle of the
machine.

In the second arrangement, a pendulum is connected to a
toothed lantern wheel, which tends to turn in one direction,
and is held between projecting pins on the surface of two

segments keyed to a shaft. On the pendulum swinging out of the vertical position, it throws the lantern wheel towards one segment, thus freeing it from the other and turning the segment. The shaft is thus turned, which in its turn actuates rudders for controlling the machine.

(*Drawings.*)

A.D. 1891. No. 16033.

GRIFFITHS, Thomas, and BEDDOES, Thomas Henry Willoughby.

" BALLOON."

An aërial raft is composed of a closed or covered vessel having a convex under surface, and a flat or concave upper surface.

Tubular chambers are attached to the upper part of the raft and filled with gas to give buoyancy to the apparatus.

A well, constructed of lattice work, is formed in the centre of the vessel for the accommodation of the aëronaut, and the apparatus is propelled by the reaction of escaping jets of fluid.

(*Drawing.*)

A.D. 1891. No. 19228.

MAXIM, Hiram Stevens.

" FLYING MACHINE."

This specification refers to improvements on a previous patent No. 16883, A.D. 1889, by the same inventor.

The chief objects of the invention are, to improve the construction of framework, to increase the efficiency of the boiler and the engines, and to maintain the machine on an even keel.

The frame of the machine is constructed of metal tubes braced together, the aëroplane being connected to the floor carrying the generator by two main side trusses and transverse tubes and stays.

Rudders situated at the bow and stern are connected together by crossed wires, which cause them to move simultaneously with a common effect, both tending to guide the machine either up or down ; and these rudders may be actuated by a cylinder which is automatically controlled by a gyrostat.

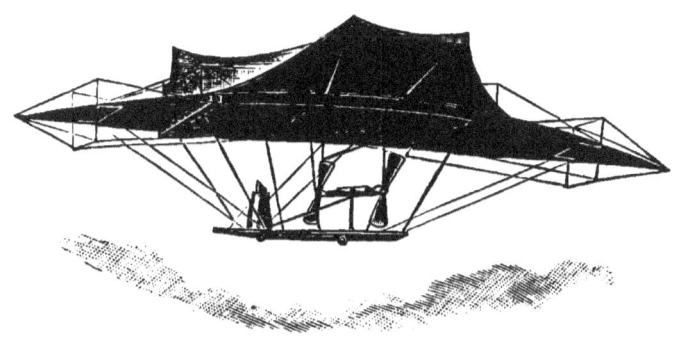

The steam from the exhaust is fed to a condenser situated in the aëroplane, the fluid returning to a force pump, which resupplies it to the generator.

A tubular generator is described, in which ether or gasoline is employed instead of water ; and engines for driving the propellers are also described.

The screw propellers are two-bladed, and are built up of strips of wood cemented together and strengthened by metal clamps or flanges.

There are 32 claims and 12 sheets of drawings to this specification.

A.D. 1891.   No. 19245.

BREWER, William John.

" NAVIGABLE BALLOON."

AN elongated balloon is enclosed in a framework, and a car having side aëroplanes is suspended below.

142

Propellers are mounted vertically above the balloon on the framework for altering the altitude, and horizontal propellers are employed for steering.

Seats are arranged in the framework to enable the aëronauts to leave the car and let same fall from the balloon in case of accident, thus dispensing with much weight.

(*Drawing.*)

A.D. 1891.   No. 20032.

HUTCHINSON, William Nelson.

" Balloons."

A LONG steel tube passes longitudinally through a balloon and serves the double purpose of a " back-bone " and a steam condenser for the generator.

A.D. 1891.   No. 21580.

LE COMPAGNON, Armand, FAUCILLON, Zélie (Vve), DUBOIS, Georges Joseph Prosper, and ROYAUX, Emile Aleide.

" Navigable Balloon."

AN elongated balloon, preferably composed of several compartments, is enclosed in a framework, which enables the whole apparatus to move steadily through the air.

The propeller, wings, or screw-blades are fixed to the sides of the framework, and are preferably actuated by a gas-engine supplied with gas from the balloon itself.

The car, which is formed of a light rectangular structure, is fastened to a shaft hanging from the balloon frame and is held in position by stays.

(*Drawing.*)

A.D. 1891.   No. 21885.

MIDDLETON, Henry.

"Flying Machines."

One, two, or three pairs of wings are employed to sustain
and propel the machines mentioned in this specification ; but
as the inventor does not confine himself to the particular
description of one machine, it is impossible to describe the
numbers of machines and their modifications in a work of the
concise nature of this volume.

A screw propeller is sometimes employed to assist in
propelling the machines.

In some of the machines the engines which actuate the
wings are rocked on trunnions, to impart a to-and-fro motion
to the wings.

Several kinds of tubular and other steam generators are
mentioned, and a generator having air heated by chemical
combination with some liquid or solid is also vaguely
described.

There are 10 claims to this rambling specification.

(Drawings.)

NAME-INDEX.

Brion, S. L.	3996	1874
Brooman, R. A.	591	1864
„ „	2030	1864
Brown, D. S.	155	1852
„ „	2529	1861
„ „	411	1872
„ „	2346	1873
Browne, F. W.	3058	1874
Browne, J.	12452	1849
Browne, J. C.	4279	1873
Bruce, E. S.	5854	1885
Buchanan, J.	327	1876
Buckhan, W. P.	1569	1879
Buckner, M. L. S.	4618	1885
Burchell, W., and another	9472	1885
Butler, J. W.	1143	1866
„ „	2115	1867
Cairncross, S.	11455	1890
Capel, T. J., and another	430	1881
Carlingford, Viscount	2993	1856
Carmien, P. J.	867	1863
„ „	748	1864
Cave, J. O'C.	140	1875
Chambers, J. M.	6419	1889
Ciurcu, A.	8182	1887
Clair, J. E. M. J.	1581	1857
Clark, A. M.	169	1875
„ „	4618	1885
„ „	9452	1886
Clark, W.	1982	1864
„ „	3283	1865
Coignard, L.	1114	1860
Cornelius, W.	2589	1884
Courtemanche, R.	2031	1871
Couturier, C. E. F.	2030	1864
„ „	2208	1865
Cowan, R. W., and another	1827	1878
Craddock, T.	1982	1867
Craig, J.	3360	1889
Crestadoro, A.	1786	1862

Kaufmann, J. M.	....	1525	1867
Kesselor, C.	....	4104	1878
Kinnear, F. C.	....	4684	1881
Koch, G.	....	5251	1882
Lake, A. W.	....	1229	1882
Lake, W. R.	....	3058	1874
,,　　,,	....	2313	1877
,,　　,,	....	985	1880
,,　　,,	....	31	1882
,,　　,,	....	518	1883
,,　　,,	....	2057	1884
,,　　,,	....	1549	1885
,,　　,,	....	14827	1885
Lane, H.	....	15567	1887
Laroche, L. P.	....	1953	1865
Lassie, J. B. J.	....	2154	1856
Le Compagnon, A., and others	....	21580	1891
Leggo, W. A.	....	3779	1879
Lehmann, F. A., and another	....	1328	1878
Lemmon, S.	....	13901	1886
Livchak, J.	.. ..	2162	1868
Lorrain, J. G.	....	11354	1888
Lüdeke, J. E. F.	....	2028	1863
Luff, H. J.	....	2447	1854
McKee, H.	....	2979	1875
Marriott, F.	....	2827	1869
Martin, M.	....	2776	1873
Martin, T.	....	122	1881
Masey, P. E.	....	412	1868
Maughan, B. W., and another	....	4585	1882
,,　　,,　　,,	....	1552	1883
Maxim, H. S.	....	16883	1889
,,　　,,	....	10228	1891
Ménier, J. S. A.	....	1144	1874
,,　　,,	....	1690	1875
,,　　,,	....	603	1877
Mennons, M. A. F.	....	2299	1864
Michel, M.	....	1769	1869
Middleton, H.	....	9725	1888

Middleton, H.	21885	1891
Moat, W. C.	9856	1843
Molesworth-Hepworth, E. N.	7837	1886
Monteith, J.	14610	1888
Moore, R. F.	13311	1890
Morris, J. M., and another	289	1875
Morse, E. C.	4154	1873
Moy, T., and another......................	3238	1871
„ „	2808	1874
„ „	1406	1877
„ „	14742	1891
Munns, W. H.	4090	1891
Nahl, P. W.	4485	1891
Nathan, M., and another	13099	1890
Nelson, J. E.	2229	1867
Newbold, H.	4332	1878
Newton, A. V.	11212	1891
Newton, W. E.	11578	1847
„ „	2959	1863
„ „	1987	1868
Nobel, A.	11212	1891
Noble, W. H.	2827	1869
Norman, J. J.	9665	1887
Oppikofer, E.	4055	1883
Osselin, A. F.	728	1871
Otto, E. C. F., and another	14737	1889
Otto, E. C. F., Jun., and another	14737	1889
Owen, R. G.	9193	1885
Pagé, C., and another	1827	1878
Parkinson, G. S.	508	1888
Pauly, S. J., and another	3909	1815
Payne, J. W., and another	924	1877
Pearse, E. A.	2229	1879
Pellen, M.	2256	1856
Petersen, C. W.	31	1882
Phillips, H. F.	13768	1884
„ „	20435	1890
„ „	13311	1891

SUBJECT-INDEX.

———◆———

BALLOONS (*continued*).

> 4647, 5404, 8816, 11455, 13099, 21241. *1891*, 1555,
> 1943, 4090, 4485, 8142, 12403, 14742, 16033, 19245,
> 20032, 21580.

FIRE.—*1854*, 224. *1862*, 1786. *1863*, 2959. *1868*, 1815,
1881. *1874*, 1144, 3132. *1882*, 4098.

MAKING GAS FOR.—*1855*, 1136. *1865*, 930. *1867*, 466.
1872, 821. *1874*, 2821, 3831. *1875*, 289. *1877*, 924.
1878, 3228, 4104, 4332. *1879*, 594. *1882*, 31. *1886*,
9452. *1887*, 9665.

PHOTOGRAPHY FROM.—*1854*, 2447. *1863*, 2028. *1877*, 1647.
1882, 4954. *1891*, 12669.

PROPELLING BY MEANS OF JETS OF FLUID.—*1843*, 9598. *1860*,
1155. *1866*, 1497, 3262. *1867*, 2223, 2229. *1868*,
1881. *1870*, 623, 2040. *1876*, 327. *1878*, 939. *1880*,
1776, 4701. *1884*, 2057. *1885*, 9472. *1887*, 316,
5644, 8182. *1888*, 508. *1889*, 6419, 14737. *1890*,
8816, 12349. *1891*, 8142, 11212, 16033.

PROPELLING BY MEANS OF SCREWS.—*1843*, 9598. *1848*, 12337.
1856, 2154. *1861*, 2529. *1863*, 867. *1865*, 930.
1871, 2031. *1872*, 821. *1873*, 4255, 4279. *1874*,
3177, 3996. *1877*, 924. *1878*, 513, 943, 1328, 3546,
4757. *1879*, 2229. *1880*, 985. *1881*, 1195, 3401,
3691, 4887. *1882*, 4585. *1883*, 518. *1884*, 2057,
2469, 15023. *1885*, 1549, 8567, 14827. *1886*, 7837,
9452. *1887*, 8255, 11941. *1888*, 9448, 11354, 12736,
14610. *1889*, 1671, 3957, 4811, 7427, 11108. *1890*,
4647, 5404, 11455. *1891*, 4485, 19245, 21580.

PROPELLING BY WINGS.—*1815*, 3909. *1854*, 224, 1224. *1856*,
2062. *1860*, 1598. *1868*, 1666. *1877*, 924. *1885*,
5118. *1889*, 47, 6419, 13207, 14737. *1891*, 21580.

PROPELLING BY OTHER MEANS.—*1853*, 179. *1867*, 2397. *1868*,
3677. *1870*, 3272. *1871*, 944. *1873*, 4255. *1875*,
2901, 3315. *1876*, 2393. *1877*, 3814. *1878*, 1827.
1879, 3997. *1881*, 807. *1882*, 5251. *1883*, 4055.

BALLOONS (*continued*).

1884, 5621, 11994, 12503, 15023. 1885, 9472, 9585, 11158. 1887, 8386. 1888, 12736. 1889, 14737. 1890, 13099. 1891, 1555.

RAILWAYS.—1843, 9642. 1873, 2776. 1878, 4268. 1879, 1569. 1882, 4387. 1885, 7727. 1886, 1821. 1888, 4552, 14610. 1890, 13311, 15332, 15850.

REGULATING ALTITUDE OF.—1847, 11578. 1864, 748. 1865, 930. 1871, 2031. 1872, 821. 1875, 2979. 1876, 2393. 1877, 2313. 1878, 513, 1328, 1827, 2039, 4757. 1879, 2229, 3779, 3997. 1881, 122, 1195, 1710, 1879. 1882, 1737. 1884, 11301. 1888, 12736, 14610. 1889, 1671. 1890, 4647. 1891, 19245.

VALVES FOR.—1848, 12337. 1856, 2062. 1867, 3036. 1872, 3076. 1884, 11301. 1889, 18952.

WEIGHT, ADJUSTABLY ATTACHED TO.—1815, 3909. 1856, 2154, 1863, 867. 1865, 3283. 1866, 3262. 1879, 2229, 3779. 1886, 7837. 1887, 316, 8386. 1888, 5742, 9448. 1889, 47, 7427, 14737. 1890, 11455. 1891, 4485, 8142.

FLYING MACHINES.

AEROPLANES, WITH.—1842, 9478. 1848, 12337. 1852, 155. 1856, 2993. 1861, 2420. 1864, 2299. 1866, 1143, 1571, 2489. 1867, 473, 1392, 2115, 3036. 1868, 392, 1178, 2680. 1870, 1469. 1871, 3238. 1872, 411. 1873, 3309. 1874, 2808. 1877, 3974. 1881, 430, 3561. 1884, 7, 13768. 1889, 14737, 16883. 1890, 11455, 20435. 1891, 13311, 14742, 19228.

CORRECTING ALTITUDE OF, AUTOMATICALLY.—1864, 2299. 1868, · 392. 1871, 3238. 1874, 2808. 1880, 10883. 1891, 14742, 19228.

MANUMOTIVE.—1843, 9856. 1864, 2299. 1865, 1037. 1866, 1143, 1571. 1867, 1982. 1868, 1178. 1869, 1124, 1877, 3974. 1884, 2589, 14038. 1885, 9193. 1886, 7015.

FLYING MACHINES (*continued*).

PROPELLING, SUPPORTING, OR STEERING WITH

screws : *1842*, 9478.   *1848*, 12337.   *1856*, 2993.   *1861*,
1929.   *1864*, 2299.   *1867*, 1392, 2115.   *1868*, 412.
1870, 1460.   *1875*, 140.   *1877*, 3974.   *1881*, 430.
1882, 4585.   *1883*, 2264.   *1885*, 8567.   *1887*, 11941.
1889, 11108, 16883.   *1891*, 19228, 21885.

wings: *1854*, 224.   *1860*, 561, 1598.   *1864*, 298, 2030,
2299.   *1865*, 1037, 2208.   *1866*, 1143.   *1867*, 473,
1982, 2504.   *1868*, 1005, 1666.   *1869*, 1124.   *1874*,
81, 777.   *1875*, 4151.   *1879*, 2376.   *1880*, 4839.
1882, 34, 1229.   *1884*, 7, 2339, 2589, 14038.   *1888*,
9725.   *1889*, 14737.   *1890*, 13311.   *1891*, 21885.

paddles, oars, jets, or other means: *1843*, 9856.   *1854*,
1334.   *1861*, 2420.   *1863*, 3284.   *1866*, 1571, 2489.
1867, 2115, 2397.   *1868*, 392, 2680.   *1870*, 2040.
1871, 3238.   *1878*, 2421.   *1881*, 3561.   *1884*, 5621,
12503.   *1886*, 1830.   *1889*, 14737.   *1890*, 11455.
1891, 11212.

VERTICAL SCREWS FOR SUPPORTING.—*1859*, 2330.   *1861*, 1929.
1868, 412.   *1875*, 140.   *1880*, 4871.   *1883*, 1552.
1885, 9193.   *1886*, 7015.   *1889*, 3360.

KITES.

1826, 5420.   *1855*, 206, 1136.   *1860*, 3103.   *1868*, 568.
1875, 169, 2428.   *1876*, 439.   *1877*, 3814.   *1885*,
15627.   *1889*, 12320.

PARACHUTES.

1815, 3909.   *1848*, 12337.   *1863*, 2959.   *1868*, 1987.   *1875*,
3315, 2428.   *1876*, 439.   *1880*, 4701.   *1884*, 2628.
1885, 9585.   *1888*, 10937.*   *1889*, 4301, 7427, 16883.
1891, 19228.

www.ingramcontent.com/pod-product-compliance
Lightning Source LLC
Chambersburg PA
CBHW020014030726

47500CB00002B/580